STRANGE TALES OF MYSTERY AND TERROR VOL. 4, NO. 1

EDITED BY ROBERT M. PRICE **PUBLISHED BY WILDSIDE PRESS**

Strange Tales is published by Wildside Press. Entire contents copyright © 2003 by Wildside Press. All rights reserved. For more information or a catalog of Wildside Press books, please visit www.wildsidepress.com, or write to: Wildside Press, P.O. Box 301, Holicong, PA 18928-0301 USA.

THE CRIMSON WIZARD

Richard A. Lupoff

It was dark in the room even though Arlie knew it was daytime outside. A little light crept in around the edges of the window shades, and the illuminated clock face on his night table said 7:30. He smiled because he knew a train would pass on the nearby track in a little while. He always listened for the passing train, the steady clatter of its metal wheels on the tracks and the occasional piercing sound of its whistle. He could make believe he was a passenger on the train, make believe that it was carrying him away from his home and his sickbed.

Arlie's imaginary train rides were more fun at night, when he could imagine himself a passenger aboard a sleek streamliner. The train passed through a darkened, tree-lined countryside. Mountains rose in the distance, a crescent moon shone though wisps of clouds, and the towers of an ancient stone castle rose, silhouetted against the landscape.

Travel on the morning trains was more difficult. Arlie knew that most of the passengers were workers on their way to their offices or students on their way to school. Still, it was fun to pretend that he was one of them, rather than confined to his bed.

He could hear his Aunt Cora bustling in the kitchen. He knew that she would be in with his breakfast and his medicine soon. Uncle Mort and Aunt Mary would already have left for work. They got up early and took the bus to the factory where they built tanks for the army. Now it was just Arlie and Aunt Cora in the apartment.

Aunt Cora was actually Arlie's great aunt, his grandma's sister. Uncle Mort was Aunt Cora's son and Aunt Mary was Uncle Mort's wife. And since Arlie's mother was dead and his dad was fighting in the army, Aunt Cora and Uncle Mort and Aunt Mary had taken Arlie to live in their apartment.

It was mainly Aunt Cora, though, who cared for Arlie.

The apartment wasn't as nice as his house had been, but they didn't have the house any more, and a boy his age could hardly have lived there by himself alone, even if he'd been healthy.

The door of Arlie's bedroom swung open and Aunt Cora appeared, carrying his tray. Some light came in through the doorway, too. Arlie blinked. The light shone around Aunt Cora. Arlie could see her smile, see her tooth with the little golden filling in it, her gray hair tied behind her head in a bun.

Arlie pushed himself upright against the old wooden headboard, a pillow propped behind his back. Aunt Cora set the tray down on the comforter. It balanced neatly across his legs. Aunt Cora held his face between her hands and kissed him on the forehead. She muttered something in the language they used to speak in the old country. That was what she always called it, never mentioned its

- 3 -

name, just the old country.

She opened the bottle of dark medicine and poured a spoonful of it. She held it for him and he swallowed it. It tasted terrible. She screwed the top back on the bottle, gave him his pills one at a time and waited while he washed them down with a glass of orange juice.

Breakfast was a bowl of oatmeal and scrambled eggs and toast. Arlie ate as much as he could, which wasn't much, and lay back against his pillow. Aunt Cora tried to coax him to eat more, and he took another forkful of eggs. They didn't seem to have much taste, and eating made him tired.

After breakfast Aunt Cora picked him up and carried him to the bathroom. When he was ready she carried him back to his bed, took off his pajamas and gave him his sponge bath. He didn't know why it was called a sponge bath, Aunt Cora just used a warm washcloth and a dry, soft towel. After his sponge bath she put him in a set of fresh, clean pajamas, even if the old ones weren't dirty.

"You want a nap, darling?" Aunt Cora asked as she tucked him back into his bed.

Arlie nodded and slid down under the comforter. He closed his eyes and listened for the train.

He heard the distant whistle, smiling to himself in the darkened room. He knew that Aunt Cora had tiptoed out, whispering something before she pulled the door shut. He couldn't make out what she said but he didn't need to. She said that he had to get well because his daddy was in Europe fighting and Arlie had to be well and strong when he got home, after he'd beaten Hitler.

The train clattered past the apartment building. When Arlie was well he used to stand in the cement courtyard four stories below his window and watch the train go by. Now he could only listen to its wheels and its whistle, but he could close his eyes in the darkened room and see it as clearly as if he'd been standing in the courtyard watching.

He wanted to reach over to his night table and turn on the radio but he felt too tired so he just waited until he couldn't hear the train any more, then thought about other things while he waited for Dr. Goldsmith to pay his daily visit.

The visit was always the same. Arlie would hear the doorbell ring, hear the door open and close again. There would be a mumbled conversation between Dr. Goldsmith and Aunt Cora. They spoke in a combination of regular American and the Old Country language. Then Dr. Goldsmith would come into Arlie's room carrying his black doctor bag and set the bag on the bed next to Arlie.

Aunt Cora would stand behind Dr. Goldsmith while he examined Arlie. He would take his temperature, look inside his ears with a little flashlight, then make him open his mouth and say ahh while he pushed his tongue down with a flat wooden stick and looked around inside. Then he'd take his *stethoscope* out of his doctor bag and put the little tips in his ears. Arlie was pleased that he knew the word *stethoscope*. Arlie would have to lift up his pajama shirt so Dr. Goldsmith could press the icy cold metal part against his chest.

When he finished examining Arlie Dr. Goldsmith always smiled. Arlie could make out his big smile even in the darkened room. Dr. Goldsmith always hummed a little tune while be put his little flashlight and his *stethoscope* back in his doctor bag. Then he would say, "Wonderful, little man, wonderful. Keep up the progress and we'll have you playing halfback any day now. He always said the same thing.

One time, after Dr. Goldsmith left and Aunt Cora came back to stay with Arlie, he asked her what song Dr. Goldsmith always hummed when he examined Arlie.

Aunt Cora said, "Happy Days Are Here Again." She asked Arlie if he liked that song and Arlie said that he did, it was a happy song and it made him feel good when Dr. Goldsmith whistled it.

Arlie was able to reach over to his night table and turn on the radio. That was another funny thing. He got sponge baths without a sponge and the table was next to his bed all the time, not just at night, but it was still called a night table.

He heard a news report on the radio. There was a big tank battle going on someplace called the Black Forest. He figured that his father was there, driving a tank and blowing up Nazis left and right. Arlie smiled.

After the news there was a quiz show and he knew most of the answers. If he'd been a lucky contestant he could have won fifty dollars and a year's supply of canned soup, but he wasn't a lucky contestant so all he could do was listen to the radio.

Then it was time for lunch, a lamb chop and spinach and a buttered roll. Aunt Cora cut the meat off the lamb chop and popped it into his mouth bit by bit until he couldn't eat any more. He ate some spinach, too, even though he didn't like it much.

Then he had his afternoon nap, and then came the second best part of the day, time for the radio stories.

He listened to *Ace Larson Space Explorer*. Ace Larson was the captain of a space ship that went to different planets. He had a girlfriend name Betty Blanton. There were always monsters on the planets they landed on, or sometimes space pirates. Betty got captured most of the time and Ace rescued her. Once Ace got captured and the giant scaly octopuses of Venus were going to sacrifice him on a big stone idol and that time Betty rescued Ace.

Arlie couldn't remember much of what his mother had looked like, but he remembered a little. He remembered her hair was really dark and long and she wore dark red lipstick and she always smiled a lot. When he listened to Ace Larson Space Explorer he knew that Betty Blanton looked a lot like his mother. Ace Blanton looked like Arlie's father.

Today Ace Larson Space Explorer and Betty Blanton were on their way to a new adventure on the Poison Planetoid. Nobody ever went there because it was such a terrible place. All the plants were poisonous and the air was full of horrible mist creatures that looked like black ropes and twisted themselves around your throat and choked you so you couldn't breath but Jimmy and Janie Jansen, the twins whose dad was the President of Earth, had been kidnapped and were being held prisoner on the Poison Planetoid and Ace Larson Space Explorer and Betty Blanton were their only hope of rescue.

The episode ended as Ace Larson and Betty Blanton's spaceship, the *Isis*, was about to land on the Poison Planetoid.

Some mist creatures had got into the spaceship and they were attacking Ace Larson Space Explorer and Betty Blanton. They were both passing out because the mist creatures were choking them and if the *Isis* crashed onto the planet they were doomed.

After *Ace Larson Space Explorer* came *The Crimson Wizard*.

Arlie liked *The Crimson Wizard* even more than *Ace Larson Space Explorer* because he had copies of *Crimson Wizard Comics* and he could read about the Crimson Wizard's adventures whenever he wanted to.

Uncle Mort and Aunt Mary got home from work and came to see him in his room. Uncle Mort brought him a comic book today, the new issue of *Crimson Wizard Comics*, and Arlie was so excited that he had one of his spells but it went away. Aunt Cora brought him dinner, a baked chicken drumstick and some beans, and he ate as much as he could.

He had to rest after dinner but then came the best part of the day. Uncle Mort picked him up and put him in his chair. He turned on the lamp over the chair. It had a lampshade made of cloth that looked brown when the light was turned off but orange when it was turned on, and a fringe of little strings hanging all around.

Arlie's room was kept dark all the time and he had to stay in bed except when Aunt Cora took him to the bathroom, but every day after he ate his dinner Uncle Mort would put him in his chair and turn on the light for him. He was allowed to stay in the chair for an hour.

During the hour he had time to listen to two radio stories, and he always read during the stories. Aunt Mary used to be

a schoolteacher before the war and she said it was a miracle that Arlie could read one story while he listened to another one and take them both in at the same time. That was exactly the way she said it, that he took them both in at the same time.

That seemed strange to him. He listened to the radio and he read his comic books. The only thing that he took in was his food and the medicine he had to take every day, but Aunt Mary said he took in the stories.

There were different stories every night. It wasn't like the radio programs he heard before dinner. Programs like *Ace Larson Space Explorer* and *The Crimson Wizard* were on this same station every day, Monday through Friday, and the stories continued every day.

But the nighttime stories were different.

Tonight they were *Tex Wilson, Sheriff* and *Crooks Beware!*

Tex Wilson rode a famous Arabian stallion named Pharaoh who was as smart as most men. Tex always wore a ten-gallon hat trimmed with a band of turquoise beads given to him by a friendly Indian tribe for saving them from a disaster caused by Snake Williams who wanted the oil that was under the Indians' land. Snake Williams had miscalculated and used too much dynamite, trying to get the oil to the surface, and instead wakened a long-dormant volcano that sent rivers of red-hot lava pouring down its sides.

The hero on *Crooks Beware!* was Homicide Sergeant Jack Martin. Jack's boss was Lieutenant Gibson, and his best friend and confidant was the lovely Marguerite Moran. Tonight Homicide Sergeant Jack Martin tackled the case of the terrible termagant. Arlie didn't know what a termagant was but it made a scary noise that sounded something like a person's voice but wasn't, and it took all of Homicide Sergeant Jack Martin's skill and courage, plus the help of the lovely Marguerite Moran, to defeat the menace.

Then your announcer Larry Thorson signed off with those familiar words, "Don't forget to tune in a week from tonight, same time same station, for another thrilling episode of *Crooks Beware!* Uncle Mort came back and picked Arlie up and took him to the bathroom, then tucked him in his bed again and turned off the light.

Arlie closed his eyes. He lay in bed, listening to Aunt Cora and Uncle Mort and Aunt Mary talking in the living room. He could hear their voices and make out a word now and then, sometimes a regular American word and sometimes a word in the Old Country language, but he couldn't tell what they were saying, not really. Except that he heard his own name once in a while.

He tried to stay awake but he was too tired and he fell asleep. He didn't have any dreams. But then he woke up when he heard a train going past. He looked at the clock on his night table and it was really, really late at night. He couldn't hear Aunt Cora or Uncle Mort or Aunt Mary, he could only hear the click of the train's wheels getting louder, then the whistle sounding exciting in a kind of sad way, then the wheels getting quieter again, and then the train was gone.

But Arlie was awake now.

He pushed himself upright, the pillow behind him. He pulled the comforter up because he felt cold. He looked in the corner of his room. There was a radiator there, and sometimes when it got too cold in the apartment and there was no heat coming up Aunt Cora would get a hammer out of the kitchen drawer and bring it and bang on the radiator.

"That will let the super know we need some heat," she always explained to Arlie. He knew that "super" wasn't short for Superman or Super Mouse or Super Rabbit, it was short for superintendent, the man in the basement of the apartment building who sent steam up through the radiators.

Next to the radiator was the darkest part of Arlie's room. In the daytime, with even a little light coming around the window shade, Arlie could see that there was just plain, dark, blank wall there.

At night the wall was even darker there, darker than any part of Arlie's room. In fact he could see that there was an opening in the wall. It led to a tunnel. The tunnel was very dark, but there were lights far away inside the tunnel. Arlie could see the light places inside the tunnel. He could see people in there and other things too.

He could see Tex Wilson and the great Arabian stallion Pharaoh. Tex was sitting on Pharaoh's back. Arlie could see Tex's lariat hanging from the pommel of Pharaoh's saddle, and Tex's glittering silver six-shooter in Tex's holster.

Tex was waving to Arlie and saying something that Arlie couldn't make out no matter how hard he tried. He leaned forward in his bed, trying to hear what Tex was saying but it was no use.

Finally he saw Tex turn Pharaoh away and they galloped off across the great open plains in search of adventure. Arlie slid down in his bed, pulled the comforter up to his chin, and fell asleep.

• • •

The next morning Arlie was still asleep when Aunt Cora came to check on him before breakfast. He found himself with her arms around him, his face pressed against her house dress. When he said, "Ouch, you're squeezing me too hard," Aunt Cora laughed and squeezed him even harder before she let him go.

She took him to the bathroom, brought him back to bed, gave him his sponge bath, and dressed him in fresh pajamas. Today's pajamas had little baseball players all over them.

He took his medicine and ate some breakfast, part of a pancake and a slice of bacon. Then Dr. Goldsmith arrived and examined Arlie the way he did every day. He didn't smile exactly the way he did most days. He did say, "Keep it up and you'll be playing halfback one of these days," but when he left Arlie's room with Aunt Cora he wasn't even humming "Happy Days Are Here Again."

Dr. Goldsmith and Aunt Cora talked for a long time, mostly in Old Country language, before Dr. Goldsmith left. Aunt Cora opened the door of Arlie's room partway and looked in at him. He lifted his hand and waved to her. She didn't say anything, she just closed the door. Arlie thought that was odd.

Even with light coming from outside around the window shade, it seemed that the dark place on Arlie's wall near the radiator was especially dark today. Arlie looked into the dark place as hard as he could. He wasn't sure if he could see the tunnel. He knew there were no lights inside. Still, this was the first time he'd even thought he might see the tunnel in the daytime.

He reached over and turned on the radio but he fell asleep before he could hear the news.

When Arlie woke up Aunt Cora was sitting on a wooden chair next to his bed watching him. He could tell it was afternoon by the way the light came around the window shade. He asked Aunt Cora if it was lunch time and she said that it was, yes, and what would he like for lunch?

He said a cheeseburger on a roll and French fries and Aunt Cora said she would make that for him and he heard her for a while in the kitchen. He could smell the food cooking and while Aunt Cora made his lunch Arlie tried to see the dark place again and see if he could make out anything inside the tunnel but there was too much light in the room.

A train went by, though, and he was able to make believe it was taking him to the Black Forest where would ride in his father's tank and blow up Nazis. Then Aunt Cora brought his lunch and he ate part of it. He asked his Aunt Cora what she was having for lunch and she said the same thing he was, he didn't eat so much and there was enough left for her.

In the afternoon he made believe that he was in a Crimson Wizard story with the Crimson Wizard. The Crimson Wizard wore a big hat with a point on top and a wide brim that hid his face from his enemies so they wouldn't learn his secret identity and attack him when he wasn't in his Crimson Wizard identity. Nobody ever saw the Crimson Wizard's face because he could never tell when an enemy might be lurking nearby, even when he was at home or in his secret lair working on a new and more potent potion or spell.

Arlie imagined that the Crimson

Wizard needed an assistant and that he asked Arlie to be his assistant. They might even change the name of the comic book from *Crimson Wizard Comics* to *The Crimson Wizard and Arlie*, and Arlie would get to share the Crimson Wizard's adventures in the comics and on the radio, too.

He had his nap and when he woke up he could tell that it was getting dark outside. He turned on the radio and listened to *Ace Larson Space Explorer* and to *The Crimson Wizard*.

Ace Larson managed to unlock the emergency equipment kit on board the *Isis* and get out oxygen masks for himself and for Betty Blanton. Once they had their oxygen masks in place Ace Larson Space Explorer was able to land the *Isis* safely on the surface of the Poison Planetoid.

But that was just the beginning of Ace Larson and Betty Blanton's latest and most exciting adventure. Ace Larson asked Betty Blanton to look outside and see what kind of place the *Isis* had come down in. Ace Larson meant that Betty should look outside through one of the *Isis*'s portholes but Betty didn't understand and she opened the hatch. A dozen scaly monsters rushed through the doorway, ray-rifles blazing, just as the day's episode came to an end.

The Crimson Wizard was facing his arch foe the fiendish Dr. Mephisto. Not only was Dr. Mephisto a powerful black magician in his own right, he knew the secret that it took to summon up all the Demon Horde of Hades. It wasn't easy for him, he could only do it when the stars of the Pleiades were in perfect alignment and the forces of good were at a low ebb. But as the Crimson Wizard himself was all too aware, the forces of good were busily engaged in defeating the Axis powers in Europe and Asia, so they were not available to aid the Crimson Wizard in holding off Dr. Mephisto and the Horde of Hades.

Arlie knew that the Horde of Hades were shown in one of the stories in his newest Crimson Wizard comic book. The radio dial gave off a little light and Arlie turned the pages, looking for the Horde of Hades. He found the story and lay in bed studying the drawings while he listened to the radio. He knew how the story came out in the comic book but it might be different on the radio. He liked the Crimson Wizard's voice on the radio. Whenever the Crimson Wizard spoke there was an echo in his voice. It sounded like the Crimson Wizard was far away and up close at the same time.

When the story ended on the radio Arlie lay in bed trying to see into the tunnel in the corner but all he could see was a black place.

Soon he heard a key in the doorway of the apartment. He remembered when he was stronger and could go out of the apartment. He played stickball with some other kids in the cement courtyard outside the building, the same courtyard where you could see the trains when they went past.

He used to walk to school, too. He walked with his best friend. His best friend was named Buddy Bill McIlhenny.

The McIlhennys lived upstairs in another apartment. Buddy Bill lived there with his mom and dad and two sisters. Arlie wished he could live with his own mom and dad and sisters instead of his Aunt Cora and his Uncle Mort and Aunt Mary but he knew that could never be. He didn't have any brothers or sisters and his mom was dead so he knew he would never have any but at least he knew his dad was in the Black Forest fighting Nazis and when he came back from the war Arlie would live with him.

When Arlie first got sick and couldn't go to school or play in the courtyard Buddy Bill visited him almost every day. They traded comic books and talked about school and the war and Buddy Bill's sisters and their other friends. But Arlie got sicker and Buddy Bill didn't visit him as often as he did at first and then he stopped visiting him.

It was wintertime now. Last winter Arlie and Buddy Bill had made a snowman in the courtyard but this winter Arlie had not been able to go outside at all. He couldn't even get to the window and look down into the courtyard to see if Buddy Bill had made a snowman without him.

He knew what the hallway looked like and he remembered the smell in the hallway and on the stairs. Some apartment houses had elevators in them but Arlie's house didn't have an elevator so you had to walk up and down flights of stairs when you went out or got home. But Arlie hadn't been out of the apartment in a long time.

He heard the door open and he knew that Uncle Mort and Aunt Mary were home. He heard their voices and Aunt Cora's talking in the Old Country language.

The door of his own room opened and Uncle Mort and Aunt Mary came in together. Aunt Mary knelt next to Arlie's bed and put her hand on his forehead and her cheek against his cheek. Her hand and her face felt cool and smooth and her cheek was soft.

He could see her dark lips even in his room. The radio was still turned on and the light from the dial made Aunt Mary's face show up clearly.

He could smell her, too. There were different smells on her. He could smell her hair and her perfume. He liked the way Aunt Mary smelled. His Aunt Cora sometimes smelled of cooking and his Uncle Mort didn't seem to have a smell, but Aunt Mary smelled like sweet flowers. He tried to remember if his mom had smelled like sweet flowers but he couldn't remember. Maybe old ladies like Aunt Cora smelled of cooking and other ladies like Aunt Mary smelled like sweet flowers. Arlie thought that he would grow up and marry a lady someday and he could smell her whenever he wanted to, not just when she came and put her cheek next to his.

Aunt Mary stood up and went out of the room and Arlie could hear her voice and Aunt Cora's together. Uncle Mort came over and sat on Arlie's bed. That was nice. Uncle Mort was still wearing his overcoat and Arlie could see a few specks of snow on the shoulders of Uncle Mort's coat. There were big pockets in Uncle Mort's coat. He reached into one and pulled out a folded newspaper. He unfolded the newspaper and took something out and handed it to Arlie.

It looked a lot like a comic book but it was thicker than any comic book Arlie had ever seen. Arlie looked at the cover. There was a picture of a castle on the front, with a full moon shining behind it. In front of the castle a big white animal sat with its head thrown back and its mouth wide open. It looked like a giant dog but Arlie knew that it was really a wolf, maybe even a werewolf.

Arlie smiled. He liked the picture.

Uncle Mort asked if he could read the name of the magazine.

Arlie was annoyed. He was a good reader. He'd learned to read even before he started school, and he was one of the best readers in his class before he got sick and had to stop going to school. He looked at the name of the magazine. It was printed in big yellow letters right over the dark sky in the picture. Arlie made a face. "It says *Haunted Adventures*. January 1945. In this issue Hounds from the Hills by Eduardo del Lobo, Marcus Billingham, Joseph Lester, Clarissa Norman, twenty five cents."

Uncle Mort grinned. "You're right, Arlie. You're a terrific reader. You want to keep *Haunted Adventures*?"

Arlie opened *Haunted Adventures*. Unlike his comic books it was printed all in black words on white pages. There were some pictures but they were in black, too. He liked comics a lot and he wasn't sure that he liked *Haunted Adventures* but he could tell that Uncle Mort wanted him to say that he liked it and he wanted to please his uncle.

"It looks great, Uncle Mort."

"Think you can read the whole magazine, Arlie?"

Arlie wasn't sure about that so he didn't say anything.

"Well, you try one story and see how you do. You might want to try that Billingham. He's a good writer. Don't worry, Arlie, if you don't like it we'll go back to comics tomorrow."

Uncle Mort ruffled Arlie's hair and walked out of the room.

•   •   •

That night after dinner of spaghetti and meatballs Arlie sat in his chair with the lamp over it. He could see the dark place on the wall, but the funny thing was, the lighter the room was the less he could see of the dark place. He wasn't sure he could see the opening or the tunnel at all, and certainly not Homicide Sergeant Jack Martin or the lovely Marguerite Moran or the Crimson Wizard.

But he was able to read the story that Uncle Mort said he would enjoy. It was called "Orchids for the Bride of the Spectre." Arlie didn't know what a *Spectre* was but clearly it was something scary. In fact the whole story was scary but still Arlie liked it and he was proud of himself for reading the whole story.

It was better than anything he'd ever read in school books, and in a way it was better than stories on the radio or in the comics. That was strange, because the comic books had bright, exciting pictures in them and the radio stories had real voices and sounds like spaceships blasting off or gunshots or the hoof beats of magnificent stallions. The stories in *Haunted Adventures* magazine only had words. Why were they so good, then?

Suddenly Arlie understood. The stories in the comic books or on the radio happened outside your head and you only saw them or heard them, but the stories in *Haunted Adventures* happened *inside* your head.

Arlie realized that he liked the idea that Marcus Billingham *wrote* the story, too. He'd never thought about that before. Comic book stories and radio stories were just *there*, somehow. The stories were there and the pictures were there, the way the sky was just there and the world was just there. You didn't think about it, or if you did some grownup would say,

"God made the sky," or "God made the world."

But Arlie didn't think that God made *Haunted Adventures* and wrote the stories in it. Arlie realized with a shock that it wasn't that way at all. Eduardo del Lobo, Marcus Billingham, Joseph Lester, and Clarissa Norman wrote the stories in *Haunted Adventures*. Somebody drew the pictures in the magazine, too, and somebody made the wonderful picture of the wolf on the cover, and somebody wrote the stories in Arlie's comic books and drew the pictures there, too, and somebody wrote the stories about Ace Larson Space Explorer and Homicide Sergeant Jack Martin and even the Crimson Wizard that Arlie heard on the radio.

Suddenly Arlie felt something inside his chest, something that he had never felt before. It was warm and it seemed to be filling him up and almost pushing out of him. He knew something that he hadn't known before. He didn't know where it came from but he knew it with all his heart. He blinked and told himself that when he grew up he would not only marry a lady who wore lipstick and smelled like flowers like his Aunt Mary, he would write stories for *Haunted Adventures* magazine.

He closed the magazine and waited for his Uncle Mort to come and carry him to the bathroom and then put him in his bed. He waited for a train to come but he didn't hear a distant whistle or the click of the wheels on the tracks.

That night he woke up when a train went past. He listened for its whistle and the click of its wheels. He could tell the exact moment that the locomotive rushed past the apartment house. He imagined himself sitting in the train as it rushed past his house and carried him to the land that the picture on the cover of *Haunted Adventures* showed. He was running through the woods. The big castle rose up, he could see its towers against the bright full moon, and he could hear the rustle of creatures in the dark woods and the distant howling of wolves.

He wondered where the dark woods were. Maybe they were part of the Black Forest and he would hear the sounds of battle. There would be American tanks with big white stars painted on them and Nazi tanks with ugly swastikas and he would see his dad.

He pushed himself up in his bed.

The clock said it was after three o'clock in the morning. It must have been cloudy outside. Arlie could see just a little bit around the edges of the window shade and he could see that it was snowing. Inside Arlie's room it was the darkest he could ever remember.

He looked at the dark place on his wall and the tunnel was there and the entrance to it was wide open. Arlie leaned forward and looked into the tunnel as hard as he could.

He could see different colored lights inside. There was a bright yellow light and he could see Tex Wilson and his mighty stallion Pharaoh. There was a dark purple light and he could see Ace Larson Space Explorer and his companion Betty Blanton standing on the surface of the poison planetoid next to their spaceship the *Isis*. There was a blue light and he could see Homicide Detective Jack Martin and the lovely Marguerite Moran; Detective Martin was wounded and he was leaning on the lovely Marguerite Moran who had a gun in her hand and was shooting at a crook.

And there was a crimson light, the strongest light of all, a beautiful crimson light and there was the Crimson Wizard and Arlie could see a little under the edge of the Crimson Wizard's hat and he was almost sure that the Crimson Wizard's face was his father's face.

The Crimson Wizard was looking right at Arlie. He spoke to Arlie and his voice was a lot like Arlie's dad's voice, but it was also a lot like your announcer Larry Thorson. He was gesturing to Arlie, too, and he was telling him that he could come into the tunnel and they would have an adventure together. The insidious Dr. Mephisto was up to his old tricks again and Arlie could help the Crimson Wizard defeat the Demon Horde of Hades.

Arlie couldn't get out of bed to go to the tunnel. He couldn't get out of bed at all without somebody picking him up, his Aunt Cora or his Uncle Mort or some other grownup. He tried, though, and all of a sudden he could move. His arms and legs didn't exactly work right, it felt more as if he was leaving his body right in the bed, right under the comforter, and he could kind of float toward the tunnel.

The Crimson Wizard was gesturing to him and Arlie was moving slowly toward the tunnel. He was near the end of his bed now, and then even though his room was really dark he could see the copy of *Haunted Adventures* there, with the picture of the wolf and the castle on the cover and the stories inside it by Eduardo del Lobo, Marcus Billingham, Joseph Lester, and Clarissa Norman. Somehow Arlie knew that if he went into the tunnel with the Crimson Wizard and his other heroes he would never come back. He would never get to grow up and marry a lady who smelled like flowers or write a story that they would print in *Haunted Adventures*.

He said, "I can't come with you, Crimson Wizard."

He turned around and he saw himself lying in bed, his head on the pillow, the comforter over him. His eyes were closed and he wasn't moving. It felt almost as if he was swimming through the air. He got back to his body and got back inside it. He pushed himself upright against the pillow and reached over and turned on the radio on his night table.

When the light behind the radio dial came on the tunnel in Arlie's wall disappeared. They were playing music on the radio. In a minute Arlie's Aunt Cora came into his room. She was wearing a nightgown and her hair wasn't in a bun, it was in a braid. He'd never seen Aunt Cora's hair like that before. Uncle Mort and Aunt Mary were behind her. They were both wearing bathrobes.

Aunt Cora ran over to Arlie and put her arms around him and he put his arms around her and hugged her and she started to cry. Uncle Mort and Aunt Mary started talking in the Old Country language. Uncle Mort went out of Arlie's room and in a minute Arlie could hear his voice, he was talking on the telephone in a voice that he always used to talk on the telephone.

Without letting go of Arlie, Aunt Cora said something to Aunt Mary in the Old Country language and Aunt Mary went out of the room and soon she came back with a tray and a glass for Arlie. Aunt Cora held it for him and he sipped at it. It was hot milk with honey mixed in it. It tasted good, Aunt Cora had made it for him before when he felt cold or couldn't sleep and he always liked it.

When Aunt Cora finally let Arlie go, he crawled to the end of his bed for his copy of *Haunted Adventures* and brought it back with him and got back under the comforter. Aunt Cora and Aunt Mary talked to each other very fast in the Old Country language.

Arlie heard the doorbell ring and heard Uncle Mort go and open it. There was more talking in the Old Country language and Arlie recognized Uncle Mort's and Dr. Goldsmith's voices. Dr. Goldsmith came into Arlie's room wearing a hat with snow on the brim and an overcoat with snow on the shoulders. He was carrying his black doctor bag.

He took off his coat and put it on Arlie's chair, then his hat and put it on top of the coat. He opened his doctor bag and took out his *stethoscope* and put the tips in his ears and the round part on Arlie's chest. It was colder than anything Arlie had ever felt, even ice cream or even snow.

Dr. Goldsmith leaned back. He looked surprised.

He took a thermometer out of his doctor bag and shook it and took Arlie's temperature.

He got one of his flat wooden things and looked around inside Arlie's mouth. He took his little flashlight and looked inside Arlie's ears. He looked puzzled but he didn't seem unhappy. He gestured to the grownups in the room and they all went out of Arlie's room but they left the door open and they took turns looking back at him.

Dr. Goldsmith stayed in the house for a long time. Arlie wondered if Aunt Cora minded Dr. Goldsmith seeing her in her nightgown with her hair in a braid but she didn't seem to.

Finally Dr. Goldsmith came back into Arlie's room and sat on the bed and looked at him again. He held his hands and looked at them, picked up Arlie's pajama shirt and looked at his tummy and his chest.

He stood up and put on his overcoat and his hat and picked up his doctor bag. He went out of the room and Arlie could hear Dr. Goldsmith and the other grownups talking again. They talked for a long time. Dr. Goldsmith came back still again and peered at Arlie.

He turned around and went to the front door. Arlie heard Dr. Goldsmith open the front door and he heard him whistling that song that Arlie liked until he heard the front door close.

A SHIP OF MONSTROUS FORTUNE

Adrian Cole

In the perpetual conflict between Light and Darkness, many battles are fought in the shadowlands between the two. The gods deploy their armies, their warriors, who move among men and shape their destinies. One such company of warriors is the Skaveen, each of them forged like a sword fit for a god, to burn through the darkest folds of night.

•　　•　　•

High above the moonlit city of Santa Varenga, a dozen watchtowers stretched across the mountain, a third of the way up its rugged side. From these stone aeries, the soldiers of the watch looked across the rooftops, splashed now with milky light, down to the distant harbour, where they could just discern the dark stains that were the moored ships of the city and the many visitors from across the sea. Far below could be heard occasional remote sounds of revelry, a surge of group laughter, a woman's shriek of mock terror, a tinkling of glass. Tonight the entire city celebrated, and when this reiver stronghold did so, it did so with gusto.

On the easternmost tower, two guards leaned over the parapet, resigned to the frustrations of a tour of duty that would end with the dawn, when the revels would have become the last glow of embers. The older and senior of the two, Arrando, nodded patiently at the seemingly miniature buildings. "They'd be ripe for con-quest this night, Elvar."

The other, a youth of barely eighteen summers, nodded restlessly. Of all the nights to be selected for duty on the towers! Why could they not have chosen someone else like Arrando instead of him for tonight's watch? The veteran, at least, had enjoyed more than his share of festivals in the past. But there was no arguing with the dictates of the Magisters, Lords of the City. "Who would dare attack Santa Varenga?"

"We are the envy of the seas," Arrando nodded. "Outside fleets court our flag. Many of them are here tonight. The promise of riches was too tempting."

"You're an old campaigner, Arrando." It was true, for the older man had spent his own youth on the decks of many a freebooter, fighting for booty and glory, though evidently he had squandered whatever he had won. "What do you know of this Treasure Ship that the entire city is getting hysterical about?"

"Most of it is legend, my boy. Loud talk to win over young men like you to crew it. Believe me, I have seen such things before. Though I will admit that the ship of the Barbaranza Brothers has a reputation like no other before it."

"They are said to be the wealthiest of the wealthy, with a hoard to match those of the remote Diamond Emperors," the boy said wistfully, as if he could see the gems glittering before him.

Arrando laughed good-naturedly. "Ah, yes, they plant the seeds of lust very persuasively when they come looking for a crew. Santa Varenga spares no efforts to encourage them. The Magisters earn a goodly percentage from whatever the takings. Last time the Barbaranza Brothers returned from a voyage, they brought a hull full of gold." But Arrando's face clouded. "Though at a price."

"The crew?"

"Over two thirds were lost. It is always so with the voyages of the Barbaranza Brothers. Some of my old friends have lost sons on those runs. So, be wary, my boy, eh? Think twice if you are considering giving up your post and going in search of glory out there." He nodded at the black, glass-like ocean.

Elvar could see that his companion had grown wistful, so he left him for a moment and walked slowly along the wall, studying the piled clouds, themselves amassing like a gigantic aerial fleet to run down the moon. Behind him he heard a sudden scuffle of movement and swung about, studying the tumbled scree from the mountain that had piled itself up against the base of the wall. In places it was almost as high as the parapet and on one such ridge he could see a shadow detaching itself. Something scampered along the rock spine, a creature a third of the size of a man, lithe as an ape.

The young man walked towards it slowly, knowing it for what it was: a rockrunner, one of the gargoyle-like creatures that inhabited the middle and lower slopes of the mountain. They occasionally slipped across the wall and over the roofs on the other side, hunting for food. Usually nervous, they came only at night and avoided human contact. This creature, though, seemed to be scurrying towards Elvar, as though he was the object of its attention.

He gently lifted his javelin, cautious rather than threatening. In a moment the rockrunner was on a ridge beyond him, peering at him with its large, oval eyes, squatting down, goblin-like. Clearly it wanted to communicate. Elvar nodded, uncertain how to react, waiting for it to speak.

"Master," it said in a surprisingly low voice, almost a growl. It looked as if one of the gargoyles in the lower temples had come to life. "There is danger."

The words surprised Elvar almost as much as the fact that the rockrunner had singled him out. "From what?" he whispered.

"I was high up on the crags. Moonshine is strong tonight. Paints the sky."

Elvar instinctively looked up at the clouds, where the huge moon did indeed invest them in a brilliant glow.

"Strange craft there," said the rockrunner, its elongated finger prodding at the packed shapes. "Saw it from the crags. Not good."

"*Craft*?" repeated Elvar. "Have you been stealing cheap wine?"

"Ship in the sky. Dark ship. Warriors. Watching city."

Elvar was about to reply tersely, dismissing the creature, but he heard Arrando's soft footfall behind him. The rockrunner did not seem frightened, making no move to flee.

"This creature," breathed Elvar, "is uncommonly brave. But its wits are addled. It says it has seen a ship in the sky."

Arrando frowned. He leaned forward

slowly. "Say, rockrunner, what is this? A ship? In the clouds. Have you been dreaming?"

The creature darted another worried look at the sky, shaking its head vigorously. "Dark ship. Warriors," it repeated. "I saw its name. On prow."

Arrando's frown deepened. "What name?"

"*Scavenger*. Like me. Like rockrunners. Its warriors watched the city."

"He's lost his wits," Elvar whispered.

The moon clouded over and darker shadows spread across the rocks and wall. As they reached the rockrunner, the little creature stiffened as if cold water lapped at it. Without another word it swung down into cover and the two guards heard a brief rattle of stones as it fled back to the crags.

"Mean anything to you?" Elvar asked his companion.

"I don't trust these rockrunners. *They* are the scavengers. We better keep a close eye on this part of the wall. It may be some trick to divert our attention, while they undertake a pillaging raid. What with the festival, they stand to gather enough scraps for a winter store."

Elvar could see, however, that Arrando was troubled. "What is this *Scavenger*? Something out of legend?"

Arrando grunted. "Aye, just that. An old legend. I haven't heard it mentioned for years. It's not common along the islands."

"A night of legends, then, what with the Treasure Ship berthed outside the harbour. At least it will help to stave off the boredom! Come, Arrando. Tell me about it!"

Arrando sighed. "No harm in that, I suppose. Well, it was once said that when

warriors died, certain of them were chosen by the gods to serve aboard the *Scavenger*, their ship piloted by the Shadow Navigator. Only the strongest, fittest could serve the gods. Those who were taken became Skaveen, the grim crew of the ship that sailed beyond worlds, beyond time. On tides of stardust they came, their deeds prompted by the whim of the unknown gods they served. Immortals, indestructible in battle, invested with power beyond imagining." He was looking apprehensively at the sinister armada of clouds as he spoke.

Elvar grinned. "And the rockrunner saw their ship, did he? A nightmare, eh? Or do you think he did see something?"

"Rockrunners keep well to themselves. They do not share our mythologies. I just wonder how he heard of the *Scavenger*."

"They're worse than vultures, Arrando. Who knows what conversations they overhear when they're scratching for food down in the city? But these Skaveen, what sort of duties did they perform for their gods?"

"What does a warrior do but fight? It was said that when they came, men died. Sometimes in great numbers."

"Well, I can see nothing but clouds. Some of them may *look* like sailing ships, but that's all."

Arrando nodded, smiling though his voice was thick with tension. "Nevertheless, we'll keep a sharp eye out this night, I think."

•   •   •

Along the waterfront, lights blazed from every window, the bars crammed with revelers, spilling them out on to the quayside. Tonight everyone enjoyed equal status, soldiery locked together with traders, pirates with soothsayers, slave-traders with priests. The Festival broke down all barriers, the wine flowed, the city danced to a kind of madness.

Out on one of the long piers that poked like a black finger into the even blacker waters of the bay, two men were sharing a bottle of wine themselves, swigging at it in turn, wiping at their chins with greasy fingers. Overhead a sputtering lantern threatened to go out, but there was enough light from the distant waterfront to see by. These men tended the moored craft at this pier, scores of them, packed as tightly as the sweating bodies in the taverns. Never before had so many ships clustered together in Santa Varenza's harbour.

"You can smell the gold lust," sniffed one of the men, a wiry fellow dressed in oilskins, his face weathered by years at sea, his eyes hawk-like.

"Uh?" grunted the other, a squat shape, hunched up on a tar barrel. "Where?"

"Not here, in the taverns. Drips off 'em like sweat. Nothing like gold to bring 'em in. The Brothers know it well enough. Serves 'em richly."

"Would you crew for 'em?"

"Nah! Sooner serve in the pits of hell. The Brothers want more than your service, more than your soul! Hah!"

The other snorted, sagging back, eyes drooping. Evidently his contribution to the slurred conversation was at an end. Oblivion beckoned him.

His companion spat into the dark water beyond the pier and shuffled along to its end, staring dazedly at the swell for a moment. Somewhere out in the bay, he could hear the dip of oars, the creak of rowlocks. He squinted, but the darkness was pitch. The harbour was no place to be tonight, with so many craft bumping and nudging each other. Best to keep the revelry to shore. He was about to hail the invisible craft, but something stopped him. He held his breath, waiting.

Out of the shadows, a long, slender prow knifed through the waters. It was an elegant, unfamiliar craft, three pairs of oars at each side, the rowers cloaked by the night, only their black backs visible. Two men stood in the prow, watching the shore like eagles, their faces limned by the distant glow from the harbour lights. One of them caught sight of the figure on the pier and waved.

"Ho, there! A berth, if you please."

The harbourman gathered his wits. "Tonight? Are you joking, man? The harbour is stuffed full. No berths here. Move away. You'll be lucky to find a quay within three miles of Santa Varenga with room."

"There's room enough for a landing," came the terse reply.

The harbourman tossed away the empty wine bottle and clumsily pulled out a cudgel, brandishing it as he spoke. "My word's law on this here pier! I say there's no room. Move away! I speak for the Magisters."

But the craft surged forward swiftly and silently, its prow touching the very end of the pier, inserted between two rougher craft that seemed to edge away from it. The two men in the prow were ashore before the harbourman could move.

"We mean no disrespect to your masters," said the first of them. He was tall, his body draped in a thin cloak against the night and sea winds, as if he had lately come from a voyage. Strapped to his back was a scabbarded broadsword.

Before the harbourman could reply, the craft had withdrawn, the oarsmen steering it back into the folds of night from which it had come. "You took a risk," he grunted, but he wavered. These men were warriors before they were sailors, and something in their manner made him shiver. There were lighter swords under their cloaks and a purpose in their gaze that shrivelled any argument.

"Might I know what your business is?" said the harbourman.

The first of the men smiled, but it was humorless, his face the cold mask of a fighting man, his eyes the knowing eyes of one who has looked on death many times. Was he, perhaps, an assassin, or a mercenary on some rebel lord's mission? His companion was no less formidable, his own steely gaze disarming.

"Like many of your celebrating populace, we seek the Barbaranza Brothers," he said, his voice flat and emotionless. "Where may they be found?"

The harbormaster scowled. There was treachery afoot. He had smelled it often enough among the pirate crews along this coast to know its pungency. "No emperor was better protected," he scoffed.

"We mean no harm," said the first of the men. He drew back a fold of his cloak and pulled coins from a pouch at his belt. The weapons that were revealed were of the finest quality. But there was something else, something woven into the fabric of the shirt. Sigils, a motif. These men were not cheap hirelings. "Here, harbourman, take this for your trouble."

The latter snatched at the three coins: they were silver and of high value. "You want the Brothers? You'll find their long-

boats two piers over. But you won't get aboard. Not unless you want to fight an army. Their emissary is abroad, though. Ask in any tavern. They'll tell you where."

"Our thanks," said the first of the cloaked men, with an incline of his head. At once he and his companion strode along the pier.

Behind them the second of the harbourmen snorted, sitting up stiffly as he realised he was not alone. He saw the two disappearing seamen and was about to shout a drunken challenge, but an arm clamped on his shoulder. "Hey! Get yer hands off me!"

"Shut your mouth, you harlot's son!" The harbourman was watching the two men as they melted into the crowd. He breathed a deep sigh of relief when they were lost to sight. "I know that livery. Where in all the hells have I seen it before?"

"Warriors? Looked like it," belched the first, slumping again.

"Aye, they're killers, those two."

"Well, let's get some of the quay rats to sort 'em out—"

"No, keep still. Get yourself another bottle. Forget you saw them. No good will come of it if we get involved." He sounded sober now, his eyes watching the bobbing ships anxiously.

"Who are they?"

"Never mind." But he knew. He had recognised the sigils on the shirt, had remembered the stories. Myths or half-truths told on long voyages to stave off the dull watches of the night. *Skaveen*. Servants of the Shadow Navigator. They were here. They were real.

And Retribution had come to Santa Varenga.

•　　•　　•

Mordruin and his companion, Scallifor, spent an hour elbowing their way through the seething crowds along the quays and side streets of Santa Varenga. The citizens were far too steeped in their revels to pay much heed to two more foreign visitors, no matter how strange their garb or forceful their nature. Ale and wine had made companions of everyone and in truth, the jostling and bustling and heaving of bodies was uniform throughout the streets. It was at its worst around one particular tavern, a notorious pirate's nest, where many a black bargain and dubious deal had been struck. It was here that the Barbaranza Brothers had sent their unscrupulous emissary, who culled the pirate ranks for a crew.

Outside the tavern, pushing their way to its very doors, Mordruin and Scallifor exchanged knowing grimaces. "This is the place," said Mordruin, shouldering his way through a number of protesting sailors, for here the opposition was strong. Those who sought a berth with the Brothers' crew were many in number. But when they looked into the eyes of the two cloaked strangers, none of them sought a fight.

Inside, the tavern was an oven, the stink of bodies a wave, the noise equally as oppressive. Everyone shouted at once, many of the men in here standing on tables, waving their arms, making it impossible to gain individual attention. Mordruin and his sullen companion pushed their way to a place where they could see the bar and Mordruin indicated that they should wait. Several burly seamen glared at them, but stood back, concentrating instead on what was happening.

At the bar, a huge barman banged down on the counter with the haft of his cutlass. Gradually the babble died down as attention focused on him. "As long as you scum go on making that row, you'll get nothing. When you've finished, our guest is are ready to begin."

There was a loud cheer, but it was cut short by the savage glare of the barman. Mordruin smiled, for controlling this mob was no mean feat. The barman jabbed with his cutlass at the air and from beside a wooden staircase, a group of men stepped forward. Unlike everyone else in the tavern, they wore uniform. It was dark green, braided, like the trappings of a royal navy, as if they served in the ranks of a monarch's fleet. Indeed, the Barbaranza Brothers were considered by more than a few to be the kings of the sea, so much power and influence did they exert over the imaginations of men.

Their leader, a swarthy fellow, with his hair tied back neatly in a tail, feathered with dark green ribbons, smiled on the assembly condescendingly. "Brothers of the seas!" he called and this was a cue for them to cheer. He waited theatrically, before going on. This was evidently a well-rehearsed speech.

"I am Zarobos, bosun of the *Sleekfin*. You know well enough why I am here. Our masters are shortly to go in search of treasure once more." Another cheer. "You know also that they are not modest in their pursuits. Death and danger sail with us always. But those treasures worth the winning incur the greatest risks. Our masters have their reputations to think of. Who else would dare the perils they dare? Who else sails into the teeth of the gods' anger? Who else brings home the fabulous riches the Barbaranza Brothers take for their own?"

"No one!" bawled the company.

Mordruin turned to Scallifor. "It's said men kill each other for a place on their crews."

"We may have to do the same," said Scallifor coldly.

Mordruin did not reply. His fellow Skaveen was no more a lover of death and killing than he was, but Mordruin had watched his inevitable transformation into the near-automaton conditioning since his first appearance on the Shadow Navigator's ship, when his charge had been given to Mordruin. Scallifor was a youth of twenty-two, but a fierce fighter, perfect machine tooled to the purpose of their terrible controller. This was their third campaign together, though the first two had been as part of a small army sent to deflect the course of a war, the outcome of which served the purposes of the gods who drove them. Dreadful conflicts, they had turned the youth into what he now was, resigned to being an instrument of destruction, blind servant of the powers. He had died and died again, as the Skaveen were doomed to die, only to rise and labor on for their grim cause.

This time there were only two of them sent out from the *Scavenger*, with instructions to join the crew of the Barbaranza Brothers at any cost. As Scallifor had said, they may have to kill for that goal.

As these thoughts played on Mordruin's mind, Zarobos studied the crowd calmly. "I have to warn you," he said, his white teeth gleaming, "that this new venture will take us into the very heart of legend, should we succeed. Oh, believe me, there is no guarantee that we will succeed. My masters grow very ambitious. This time, our goal is danger beyond danger, a dance with death, a step through hell itself."

Mordruin expected amused jeers, but a strange silence had fallen.

"I do not exaggerate. When I tell you where we are bound, you will know I speak the truth. It is the Crimson Island. We seek Fire Rubies there." He had named one of the most cursed legends known, every seaman's nightmare.

Silence hung like a cloud for only a moment. Then someone broke it with a rude shout. "'Tis a jest! Only madmen would venture to such a place. Those who have tried in the past are food for the worms in the sea bed, or worse!"

Others joined in the general dissent.

"Come, Zarobos! Give us the truth. Where are your masters *really* bound for?"

The bosun studied them with measured deliberation, pursing his lips in a stare of disapproval. "I did not come here to waste time in *jest!*" he hissed. "I have said. Our course is set for the Crimson Island. I need fifty men. If not from Santa Varenga, then from some other port where stomachs are stronger and spirits not withered by too many soft nights."

It was a signal for many of the company to leave, for the terrifying stories that gathered about the Crimson Island and its hell-spawned rubies were enough to dent the hardiest resolve. There were whispers that the Brothers had at last overreached themselves, perhaps gone mad. Even so, a large body of men remained, although the mood had changed, the faces were suddenly more drawn, ripples of fear eddying like currents among them.

Zarobos and his fellows seated themselves at a table and began listening to the first seaman who gabbled reasons for wanting to be selected. Mordruin watched the bosun as he occasionally nodded his head, his eyes fixed, expression unreadable. At length there was an opportunity for Mordruin and Scallifor to speak.

The bosun eyed them with candid interest. "You have the look of wealthy men. Whom do you serve?" he asked bluntly.

Mordruin spoke for them. "Ourselves now, bosun. Lately we were part of the retinue of a certain northern monarch. We did well enough in his house. Sadly, however, he had two nephews who had never quite reconciled themselves to his taking the throne. Consequently they drew up an army, the numbers of which significantly outnumbered the corresponding army of the monarch. He was deposed after a particularly violent rebellion. Some of us were perceptive enough to foresee the outcome, hence the appearance here of my companion and I."

"There is no room on the *Sleekfin* for soft-bellied, land-hugging sycophants," said Zarobos with a sniff. "Have you ever *been* to sea?"

Mordruin smiled at the insult. Beside him Scallifor was motionless. But he had been trained well. "Indeed. The sea holds no fears for me. Nor does your island of blood."

"What were you at court? You speak the way a chamberlain would talk. And is this youth your eunuch?"

Again Mordruin smiled, but there were only a few uneasy laughs in the hall. "You mistake me, bosun. My companion and I are soldiers. Before that, I sailed and fought at sea, many times. Death is no stranger to me, nor to Scallifor. And I promise you, he is no eunuch. Lesser men

than you have insulted him, though none of them could verify it now."

Zarobos's eyes were slitted like those of a serpent, as if he might unleash a physical challenge. But he simply nodded. "Well, you know that many men seek to impress my masters. Perhaps I will keep you in mind."

Mordruin bowed. He and Scallifor walked away to a place in the tavern that was less crowded, for even more of the original throng had departed and the word had gone out into the city that the Barbaranza Brothers were intent on the maddest of ventures.

"Will he take us?" said Scallifor as Mordruin waved another barman to them.

"He'll have to. On this quest, he'll be lucky to pull half a crew."

•　　•　　•

Mordruin's words were to prove an accurate prediction. In the early hours, before the first hint of dawn, a longboat pulled away from the quayside and out into the bay. Apart from the dozen men who worked its oars and the bosun at the prow, it contained two dozen others, those who had been selected to serve aboard the Barbaranza ship. In the darkness nearby, a sister longboat slid through the inky waters. Mordruin and Scallifor sat in the first, listening to the muted conversations around them.

"No regrets then, Ulvars?" came a gruff voice nearby. "You don't fear the Crimson Island?"

"Course I do. Anyone who says he doesn't is either lying or a fool! But a man can rot in Santa Varenga for want of something to do, especially with no money. No, Trennick, I'll take my chances with the Brothers."

"They say they're a queer pair. Best team on the oceans, but they can't stand the sight of each other."

"Yeah, I heard that. Whatever mother gave them life, cursed them at birth. Some say they fought in the very womb."

Another voice cut in from the shadows. "Some say they won't even stand beside each other. For twins they're as unalike as wine and water. Argangulis is long and thin, while Uttarsung is like a whale!"

The figure at the prow turned, moonlight playing across its scowling face. "Save your comments. The Brothers have keen hearing. You'll meet them soon enough." He was limned now against a backdrop of sky and sea and the long, sleek lines of a ship. Mordruin studied it silently as it rode at anchor. It was narrow, its masts oddly short and tipped back, the sails limp in the still air. It seemed to him more like a great fish than a craft, as if imbued with life of its own. Two banks of oars protruded from its side like long fins, and Mordruin wondered how many men pulled at those powerful blades.

Soon afterwards the longboats disgorged their passengers and were hauled aboard the parent craft. Zarobos indicated the narrow deck. "We sail with the dawn tide. You'll receive your orders then. Get some rest. Any questions?"

No one was inclined to ask and with no further ado, Zarobos went to the cabins aft of the deck The fifty men who had joined the ship made themselves as comfortable as they could, used to cramped conditions at sea, most of them being veterans, hard-bitten and battle-worn. They were at home here, even more so on the storm-tossed waters of the oceans, one with them.

Mordruin and Scallifor sat together, quietly weighing up the craft around them.

"Strange vessel," said the youth. "There are few crew members. Oarsmen below. Unless the ship is powered by similar forces to those that pull the *Scavenger* through astral seas."

Mordruin frowned at the reference. He had never seen the below-deck crew of the Shadow Navigator's craft, though knew it to be supernatural. "We're here because the Brothers call upon dark powers. I'd wager few of her previous crews survive to talk about their exploits. Whatever the Brothers are involved in, the Navigator does not condone it. Their black sorcery must end."

Scallifor knew better than to persist in questioning his leader. Mordruin was a singular man, who spoke little at the best of times, his thoughts private. It was true of many of the Skaveen, for most had lived troubled lives, ending in pain, sometimes dishonor, before they had chosen to kiss the Skaveen blade and become part of the Navigator's sombre crew.

When dawn's light washed the horizon, the ship shuddered into life, those great oars working in unison to urge the craft across the bay in a smooth, flowing motion. Most of the crew had been asleep, able to drop off whenever a chance came. Now they stirred as one, the hubbub of their voices growing, a buzz of excitement fuelled by the thrill of the quest, the lure of treasure that had wooed men like them for countless generations. As the ship seemed almost to flow across the bay, there was movement on the high rail at the stern. Every eye turned. The bosun was there, and beside him, one of the fabled Barbaranza Brothers.

This was Argangulis, every inch as tall and skeletal as he had been described. Almost cadaverous, with extraordinarily thin arms and legs, and a face that was as white and gaunt as that of a corpse. The eyes were alive, though, burning with an inner passion, studying the blur of faces below with the sharpness of a bird of prey, almost as if hungry to select a target. His bony fingers clutched at the rail as if they might splinter it, hinting at an ironic power within that spare frame.

When he spoke, the timbre of his voice was as strange as his body: it was deep and rich, soft but strong. He did not have to raise it to reach his audience and they heard every word as clearly as if it had been spoken into their ears. Again Mordruin was conscious of supernatural powers.

"I bid you welcome to the *Sleekfin*. I am Argangulis. My brother Uttarsung and I are masters of this ship and you now serve under our command. You will be well rewarded for your service, beyond anything you could possibly have imagined. You need only sail with us this once. Ever afterwards your lives will be changed. I am sure rumours of this have reached you. It is, after all, why you are here." He smiled, but it was the smile of a predator, the light that danced behind those eyes unearthly. "We expect absolute obedience in everything. We will encounter huge dangers, make no mistake. Only by uniting under us can you expect success. You will undoubtedly be required to kill for us, perhaps without warning or explanation. If such a contract is not to your taste, it is better that you leave us now." The eyes studied them all, but no one demurred.

"We do not kill for the sake of it. We only do what is necessary to guarantee our success. Good. Now, I have to tell you that my brother, Uttarsung, is unwell. It is nothing serious, but he will be confined to his quarters for most, if not all, of our outward journey. You will have the pleasure of meeting him in the future," he added, his voice laced with sarcasm.

"As for our destination, you already know it. The Crimson Island. A terrible foe. And what we seek there—well, a taste to whet your appetites." He turned to his bosun with a curt nod.

Zarobos lifted a leather bag the size of a fist and made a show of undoing its thong. Argangulis held out his palm and Zarobos emptied from the bag a brilliant red stone. It glowed and pulsated like a living organ, the early sun's rays scintillating from it.

Argangulis held it aloft for all to see. "Each of these Fire Rubies is worth an emperor's treasury. With those we take from the Crimson Island, we shall attain riches undreamed of by man before." His fingers closed around the jewel, slipping it back into the bag.

The crew was rigid with amazement. "He's right! That jewel alone must be worth a fabulous sum," someone breathed. There were murmurs of assent.

"The *Sleekfin* has a long journey, but for now she moves under the power of her oars. When we encounter enough wind, then we'll test your seamen's skills. A last thing, you'll want feeding. No one goes hungry on this ship," he laughed softly. "Take what you need. Keep yourselves in readiness." He nodded stiffly then moved away, his gait awkward.

Scallifor leaned over to Mordruin. "Are these Brothers human?"

Mordruin frowned, his implications clear.

•　　•　　•

Several days passed, merging into one long, slow period, when there was little to do but watch the empty horizons, broken now and then by the passing of another ship or small fleet. Patience ruled the crew, but they were professionals. They passed the time by keeping themselves fit, scrambling up the rigging like apes, or wrestling or mock fighting with cutlasses and dirks. Mordruin and Scallifor joined them at this, careful not to overplay their skills, for both were far superior in the use of weapons. Astute members of the crew guessed this, but they were glad enough to have such skill in their company. Time enough for its proper use later.

One night, when most of the crew was either asleep or drowsing, Mordruin was studying the still calm seas at the rail. Silently Zarobos joined him.

"You are to come with me," said the bosun and led the way below. The quarters were even more cramped, timbers groaning and creaking to the sway of the speeding ship. Zarobos paused outside an unusually wide cabin door. He tapped on it and a muffled voice responded. Zarobos motioned Mordruin inside.

The cabin was also peculiarly wide, the low beams forcing Mordruin to bow his head. Opposite him was a long glass portal overlooking the sea astern of the ship, its foaming wake. He looked around to see who was in here, but there were several thick curtains along one wall. Zarobos pressed close behind him and he sensed that the bosun had drawn a blade. Tensing, he prepared for treachery. Had they recognised him as a Skaveen?

"Mordruin," came a voice from behind the curtains. "I am Uttarsung. Pardon my modesty. I am mortified and not a little embarrassed to say that sickness confines me to my bed." If Argangulis's voice had been low, this was even more so, a controlled *basso profundo* that resonated even though it was hardly above a whisper. Yet it gave an impression of abnormal *size*.

"I am sorry to hear this."

"I appreciate your concern. It has been communicated to me that you and your companion are gentlemen, not at all like the flotsam and jetsam of the rest of the crew, worthies though they are."

"Even gentlemen fall on hard times," Mordruin said cautiously. "Without a fortune of some description, Scallifor and I would be reduced to a more lowly existence."

"Of course," purred the extraordinarily deep voice. "But I have not called you here to carp at your manners. I applaud them. No, I simply wish to say that, when we reach Crimson Island, I want you to lead the first party ashore. Argangulis has been weighing the crew. They are a formidable company and will need to be. You, I think, are best fitted to lead them."

"What manner of opponents will we face, if I might ask?"

"We cannot be certain. You know that the Island has an awesome reputation. Some say these monsters are alive. Certainly it migrates in the way that other creatures of the sea do. The reason we are pressing an assault now is that it has drifted further north than usual. The waters in which it has anchored itself are colder. It will have become more sluggish, as it hibernates. We have studied its patterns and the timing of its cycle.

"It will defend itself. We will have little time to take what we seek. But we know where the Fire Rubies are." The voice rose slightly at mention of the jewels, a hint of excitement bubbling from its depths, redolent with greed.

"I did not come on this venture to withdraw at the first stab of danger," said Mordruin. "I'll lead your party."

"Excellent. We'll not speak again until we arrive. Be patient. The rewards— ah, Gods of the Deeps, the *rewards*!"

A nudge from Zarobos confirmed that the interview was at an end. Mordruin could feel the presence behind the curtain and nodded, assuming that he could be seen.

Back on deck, he repeated to Scallifor what he had been told. "If the Brothers suspect we are Skaveen, they have given no sign of it. They have no reason to think our story is false. Their fabulous wealth is well known. I imagine they have attracted warriors of repute to them before now. I am only surprised that none of them have remained."

"That surprises me, too," said Scallifor. "Why do their crewmen serve only once? The best crews, the best warriors, are those with the most experience. Those you can rely on."

Mordruin nodded. "Especially when your quests grow more and more demanding. This quest flies in the face of reason. It would be better crewed with men who had sailed on the *Sleekfin* for years. Still, it will suit us better to lead them ashore."

• • •

Late one afternoon, Mordruin and Scallifor were watching the sluggish movement of the waves around them. They were hundreds of miles from land but the sea here was a bright green in colour, thickened to a soup by kelp spores. On the breeze there was a scent of decaying vegetation, as if a hidden weed reef had been exposed to the heat of the day. The ship had sailed into semi-tropical waters, the midday temperatures soaring now, even the seas reflecting the glare of the sun like burnished metal. The crew grew restless, eager for activity. Tempers flared in the endless training exercises.

Mordruin turned to find himself looking into the strange gaze of Argangulis, who had rarely ventured on to the deck during the journey.

"I understand from my brother," he said, somehow infusing the word with a bitter coldness, "that you have been chosen to lead the shore party."

Mordruin nodded.

"I was not consulted about this."

"I made no special plea. Chose another if it suits you better."

Argangulis shook his head, cruel eyes studying the sea. "No, you will suffice. Now is not the time to be in dispute with my brother. What do you know of Crimson Island?"

"Very little. I gather it is imbued with unusual life."

Argangulis's eyes widened. "Yes. It is certainly alive. During this fierce daytime heat, it will be torpid, barely alert. It is when we will go ashore. We avoid the night. We must be back on the ship and far from the island during darkness. This coming night we rest. Shortly after dawn, the Crimson Island will be visible. Have the men ready." He turned away without another word, cold and dismissive.

Zarobos, who had been nearby, was about to leave also, but Mordruin pulled him gently aside. "A peculiar team, these Brothers," he commented.

"Perhaps. But they recognise the advantages of their partnership. It has served them well." The note of warning in his voice was not lost on Mordruin.

• • •

During the night, Mordruin woke to find Scallifor gone from where he had been sleeping and rose softly to see him again at the rail. He went to him, careful not to wake any others of the crew, though they slept with the typical ease of sailors on a voyage.

Scallifor pointed to the dark waters, which remained like glass. "There have been several movements. At first I thought there were sharks or some other large fish out there. But I'm not so sure. More like eels, though I imagine eels that size would be exceptional."

"Squid, perhaps," said Mordruin. "They come to the surface. I gather they can be huge. Some have been known to attack ships."

"Whatever they are, they know about the *Sleekfin*. I think they follow us. With the Crimson Island so close, it would not be a good time to be in the water."

Mordruin nodded and they spent the rest of the night watching, dozing on and off. Apart from a few white bubble trails, they saw no further evidence of the sea denizens.

At first light there was a shout from the lookout, perched atop the mainmast. "Land ho! Directly ahead! Land ho!" The entire crew massed at the prow to study the horizon and minutes later the keenest eyes confirmed what the lookout had seen. A hummock of land, rising to a rounded apex lifted from the calm seas and even at this distance it was a deep red in colour. Unquestionably it was the Crimson Island. Beneath them, the men felt the ship surge, the oars striking the water and propelling the craft forward at a stunning speed, as though the ship were being *pulled* by a submarine force to its destination.

Argangulis was aft, calling out orders. "Make all haste!" he called. "Every mo= ment will be precious. Whatever transpires, we must be off by nightfall. Either that, or you will never leave the island."

Mordruin walked among the men, checking that they were properly prepared for an assault. They were a mixed lot, but every one of them was used to a leader on such an expedition and Mordruin had, during the voyage, impressed them with his qualities as a warrior and commander. Though some of them treated him sourly, all were prepared to follow instruction. The prize was too valuable to jeopardise. Rivalries and squabbles would wait until they were back in Santa Varenga.

The power of the invisible rowers below deck took the ship to within a mile of the coast of the Crimson Island well before noon. It held its position, the ocean bed too deep for an anchor, its oars dipping and gently working to keep the craft as still as possible. Argangulis motioned for the longboats to be lowered, taking his position in the prow of one of them, with a crew of oarsmen ready for the run to the island. Mordruin, Scallifor and two dozen warriors joined Argangulis's boat, weapons flashing.

"What sort of opposition can we expect?" Mordruin asked Argangulis, whose attention was riveted on the shore. "You have said very little."

"No human enemy will attack us," came the cold voice. "But the island is a living thing. If it is disturbed, it will attack us on all fronts. Its vegetation moves. You will not find the placid growths of other isles here. If we move with an easy tread and in silence, it will not stir. Fear protects it. Man's fear."

The two longboats reached a narrow bay together, mooring at a flattened area between two massed banks. Mordruin had been studying the terrain. Although most of the bizarre vegetation varied through all the hues of green and yellow, there was a taint of redness to the creepers, trees and leaves, some of which were scarlet, others a deep, velvet red. The effect was unnerving, enhanced by the unique stench of the island, reminiscent of a battlefield after blood had been spilled. The fumes of death and decay filled the atmosphere, though strangely there seemed to be no life other than the plants here: no birds, no flies. The silence that pervaded Crimson Island was that of the sepulchre.

As the warriors clambered ashore, their mood became one of deep unease. Mordruin took his lead from Argangulis, who indicated a narrow opening in the tall banks of vegetation ahead. "We must go to the heart of the island," he said. "There will be a small lake. What we seek will be on its bed."

Mordruin organized the party, putting a group of his strongest men at the rear, to watch for any unexpected attack. Satisfied that everyone was prepared, he led the way into the opening, sword held at the ready. The trailing plants were motionless, not even a breeze to stir them. Shadows closed in over the party as it penetrated the cool air of the natural tunnel. The soft pad of their feet was all they could hear, a muted cough, the brushing of an arm against leathery leaves. That cloying silence deepened, as though they were going far underground, the illusion enhanced by the height of the plants overhead, where a narrow line of blue sky thinned. Beneath them, they could feel a strange warmth, as if they trod not upon undergrowth but upon the spine of a slumbering beast, too vast to contemplate.

Gradually they rose up a long slope and the plants thinned out, the trees less tall, becoming stooped and stunted, their branches more spindly, like the gnarled limbs of crones, frozen in an attempt to pluck the warriors from the path. The men had been moving upward for an hour when they broke through into a clearing, finding themselves in an open, grassed area, overlooking a steep slope. This led down to a small lake, its waters unexpectedly pure, its bottom as clear as if viewed through unblemished glass. The lake was set in a crater, the far side of which rose up above the warriors, its brow festooned with growths, trailing down towards the water in tangled masses.

Argangulis indicated the high ridge. "I will go there," he told Mordruin. "I will see all of the island and if there is any danger, I will communicate it. You take the men down to the lake." He stabbed with a long finger at the motionless water. At its far side, under the very lip of the cliff, a livid red glow was visible. "There is our prize! The Fire Stones."

Mordruin nodded, watching his warriors. To a man, they were pointing to the treasure of the lake, faces splitting in hungry grins, like starving men who had found a banquet. But the expression on Argangulis's face held his attention more. No mere look of avarice, it was one of extreme, unbridled lust.

Before Mordruin could reflect, Argangulis slipped away along the edge of the growths, which swallowed him eagerly. Mordruin realised that the men were now all watching him. He nodded and spoke softly. "A dozen men, down to the shore below. Test the water carefully. It may look like a harlot's bathing pool, but beware of her fee."

There were many chuckles at this, and far too many volunteers. Mordruin singled out a dozen and the rest watched as they scrambled down the slope to the water's edge. They cautiously dipped fingers into the water, which was cool. Someone pushed part of a broken branch across the surface, but nothing rose to attack it. At last one burly pirate stripped off his shirt, gripped his sword in his teeth and turned to Mordruin.

The latter nodded. Instantly the pirate slipped under the surface, diving deep. Mordruin could see him clearly from where he stood, scanning the edges of the lake for any sign of hostility. But there was none. The swimmer closed with the Fire Stones and lifted one from the lake bed. In a moment he had broken surface, triumphantly holding his trophy aloft. The men cheered, but Mordruin silenced them with a sharp command. He watched the swimmer coming shoreward with long, easy strokes. As he deposited the Fire Stone on the bank, other men were diving into the lake, making for the underwater trove.

"This is too easy," said Scallifor

beside Mordruin. He would have said more, but a shout from behind them made them both turn, swords gleaming in the brilliant noon sunshine.

One of the warriors in the rearguard pounded up the slope. "Mordruin! The pathway! It has closed over. The fronds drew together like curtains. It is a trap!"

Mordruin could see the warriors down there, cutting at the verdure with their swords, but for every branch they hacked off, or thick leaf they cut in half, more shunted together, tangled, an impassable wall. As Mordruin watched the unequal struggle, new cries came from behind him, down at the lake. He ran back to study it, only to be met with a vision of unsurpassed horror. A dozen or more men were in the water, but they were no longer visible, for the water was bright crimson, *the precise hue of blood*. Streams of bubbles broke its surface.

The remaining warriors stood transfixed at the side of the lake, not knowing what to do, too afraid to take to the water in an attempt to rescue their companions. As Mordruin watched, part of the bank shuddered violently, like a carpet being shaken, and another six men were flung out into the water. It thrashed, boiling, and each man went under.

"Get away from the lake!" Mordruin bawled to the last group of warriors. They obeyed instinctively, although several of them snatched up the Fire Stones that had been retrieved from the lake bottom. Even so, three more of them slipped on the rise, slithering backwards to be snatched by something half-glimpsed and dragged into the bloody cauldron.

The company had been reduced by half and now Mordruin realised that those warriors who were attempting to re-carve a way back to the distant shore had also suffered losses as the jungle *reached out* for its victims. "Retreat!" he shouted to them, gathering the last score to him on the crest of the knoll. He could feel it heaving beneath him as though a giant was breathing, about to come to life. He looked to the far cliff top, but there was no sign of Argangulis.

"It's impossible!" gasped one of the warriors, wiping thick juices from his blade. "It replaces itself faster than we can cut it. How in all the hells do we get through it!"

"There may be a way," said Mordruin. He indicated the Fire Stones. "Scallifor, take one." He lifted one himself and went down to the edge of the trees. He could see them shivering, as though scenting him, eager for his blood. Where warriors had been snatched by them, their trunks pulsed, ominously crimson.

He lifted the Fire Stone and let the sun's rays strike it. It acted like a lens, spearing a beam of light towards the trees. Almost at once the vegetation reacted, scorched by the fierceness of the beam. It drew back, the narrowest of openings revealed. Scallifor stood beside Mordruin and mirrored his work: together they began to cut a swathe through the plants, which shook as if in a gale.

"Bring up the rear with more of the Stones," Mordruin called as he pushed forward. Behind him, two more of the brilliant Fire Stones were used. Gradually a path opened, although its sides were no longer the motionless green and red walls they had been on original entry. Now they swayed, seething as if alive with insects, threatening to probe forward. Mordruin and Scallifor pressed down the slope, but behind them they heard still more warriors shriek as the jungle took them. As they moved deeper along the path, they lost the direct sunlight, unable to use its beams to sear and char the leaves. But enough heat remained in the Fire Stones to repulse the choking plants and they used them like huge embers or torches, enough to win their way forward.

Half way down the ragged path, they found themselves cut off from the rest of the men. They could hear the crackle of fire and the continuing searing of the Fire Stones beyond the closing walls, but there were muffled screams, the forlorn cries of the doomed. Flames now leapt up either side of them and they had to hold their hands over their mouths to keep the smoke at bay.

Scallifor stumbled to his knees, and Mordruin dragged him through the last of the snatching branches to the edge of the sea. He used the sun again to focus light through the jewel, and the jungle swayed back, temporarily thwarted.

"Gods," Scallifor coughed, leaning on his companion. "Has *no one* else come through?"

Mordruin shook his head. "Argangulis has fared no better." He turned back to the water and saw the two longboats, their rowers draped silently over their oars, as if they were drugged. "Stir yourselves!" he shouted at them. "Row for your lives! The island has not done with us yet." He and Scallifor leapt into the first of the craft and at once the rowers lurched into action, pulling away from the shore without a word, heading back to the motionless *Sleekfin*.

•   •   •

By night, the ship was well away from Crimson Island. Mordruin and Scallifor had been met by Zarobos, who had insisted on taking the Fire Stones below. Mordruin had not expected him to shed any tears for the fifty or so warriors who had perished on the island, but the man's silence about Argangulis's fate seemed bizarre.

"Uttarsung insists we leave at once," he had said.

"We cannot be sure that Argangulis is dead."

"We obey Uttarsung now." There had been no further discussion.

At the rail, watching the moonlit horizon where the Crimson Island had now disappeared from view, Mordruin again slipped his slender weapon from its sheath. "Our work is almost done. You must protect my back once more."

"You fear another attack?"

"It is time to finish the Shadow Navigator's work. I must go below. It will be the hardest part, but we have to do this." He told him in level tones what had to be done to bring this grisly business to a close. Mordruin's eyes met those of the young man, a brief plea for understanding in his gaze, but Scallifor nodded curtly as if without emotion.

Mordruin left the deck and went slowly down into the heart of the ship, searching for the cabin where he knew Uttarsung sheltered himself. The thick door was firm against him. He struck hard upon it with the haft of his blade. At first there was no response, then it swung open. The cabin beyond was poorly lit, a single lamp hanging from a beam. Mordruin called out.

"Enter, noble warrior," came Uttarsung's unmistakably deep voice. The curtain that had previously hidden him was down. As Mordruin crossed to the vast bed beyond it, he had his first view of the second Barbaranza Brother. The man was impossibly huge, his head like a giant fruit perched on sloping shoulders that framed a bloated, immense body, swathed in roll upon roll of blubbery fat. The gaping mouth worked like that of a deep sea denizen and in the poor light, something gleamed on its chins and on the vast chest below. No, this creature could never be called human.

"You have performed marvelously," came the resonant voice from the depths of that cavernous chest. Somehow Uttarsung seemed like a beached creature from the deeps, his flesh like the flesh of a sea creature, as if it belonged undersea. Those horrific arms flapped, hands and fingers grotesque. "Your rewards will be great."

"Where are your victims?" breathed Mordruin, though he feared that he knew.

"Not far away," Uttarsung laughed, something dribbling thickly from his lips. It had the consistency of blood. Human blood. He dabbed at it and as he studied his fingers, his expression changed to one that Mordruin had seen before. Uniquely, on the face of Argangulis. *The look of extreme, unbridled lust.*

"Argangulis did not die on the island," the warrior said. He used his blade to flick away some of the sheets, revealing a white, leathery expanse of flesh, drained of blood. It was a warrior's corpse, brought here from the island. "There has only ever been *one* Barbaranza Brother."

Uttarsung smiled horribly. When he spoke, it was with the voice of Argangulis. "Ah, you understand the cycle. As Argangulis, I hunger, month on month, luring men to their destiny. Then, after I have *fed*—" He shrugged.

Mordruin stepped forward, his weapon poised.

Uttarsung held up a fat paw. "I wouldn't. Zarobos will take your arm off before you can strike," he smiled, reverting to the deeper voice. "Although I want you alive, as one of my rowers. Only the best are—converted."

Mordruin felt the presence behind him, swiveling round. Zarobos stood there, his blade dripping.

"Your young companion died in his sleep," said the bosun. "Take consolation from the fact that he felt no pain." But a moment later his bosun's face was agape with horror, fingers spasming. From his mouth the end of another blade protruded like a steel tongue. Behind him, Scallifor tugged it free.

Zarobos toppled forward. Scallifor held up his own blade, dabbing at the slick blood. "No pain?" he breathed. "Who could know the pain *we* suffer?"

Uttarsung laughed derisively, sagging back on the mound of human pillows now revealed behind him. He was too bloated to move, a whale stranded on a reef. "Zarobos may have bungled your death, but you cannot so easily dispatch *me!*" he snorted. "You are *mine* now, mine and the island's. I am simply part of it. I am a god! Don't you realise that! Your fate is mine to cast. I spared you on the island so that you could serve me below. Your weapons are useless."

"You are a god? Then it will take the will of a god to destroy you. The will and the instrument." Mordruin reached behind him and pulled out the long broadsword, its sigils alive in the lamplight.

Uttarsung's massive form shuddered in revulsion as his eyes read the Skaveen

runes. "You serve the Shadow Navigator? That black harbinger!" He looked incredulously at Scallifor. "So Zarobos did kill you. But, as with your kind, you rose. A Skaveen trick—"

Mordruin stepped in closer and thrust home the Skaveen blade in a deep, killing strike, down through layer upon layer of fat. Uttarsung's eyes widened in final horror, his hands flapping like fins. Only when he stopped mouthing silent shrieks of pain did Mordruin pull out the blade.

"Once we reach land, we'll turn this ship into a pyre," he told Scallifor.

The deck beneath them gave an abrupt heave, as if struck by a colossal wave. The ship seemed suddenly to be churning through the waters, doubling and redoubling its speed as if it, too, had been pierced by the Skaveen blade. Mordruin and Scallifor rushed up to the deck, peering out at the darkness, where the waves rose and fell in great swells, spume flowing from them as the prow of the ship clove them apart.

Scallifor pointed and out in the darkness the thick coils of something lashed the waters, mighty tendrils lake cables.

"*The island,*" said Mordruin. "Dragging us back in its death throes. Uttarsung was its living heart. This ship is a limb! We dare not take to the sea."

From below, they could hear the coming of the invisible rowers, now released from their oars, with the grim and horrible business of revenge goading them up to the warriors, who stood back to back on the heaving deck, a blade in each hand. The first of the misshapen nightmares appeared, scarlet eyes pooling with killing madness. A shadow fell across the moon and at first Mordruin took it to be another cloud, a veil over the carnage that must surely follow, but looking up he saw the dark shape of another ship, its form unique. It was the *Scavenger*, drifting down on an aerial wind. It drew alongside, shattering the flailing oars of the Barbaranza ship, pulling rail to rail.

A cry of encouragement from the *Scavenger's* decks urged the two warriors to get aboard it quickly, but Mordruin felt Scallifor tug at his arm.

"The crew!" cried the youth. "Not all of them perished. Can we do nothing for the survivors?"

As he spoke, a small group of sailors closed with them, ready to defend themselves from the grim apparitions that were the rowers.

"Don't abandon us, Mordruin!" one of them called above the ocean's angry din.

Mordruin's face clouded. "Do you know what ship that is?" he asked them.

The last of the pirates, four of them, gazed from the horrors that closed upon them to the black ship hovering at the *Sleekfin's* rail. Two of them could not bear the thought of what the dark ship meant and abruptly turned away, rushing like madmen at the dread oarsmen. Their death was swift as the massed creatures closed over them like a comber.

The other two men, eyes bulging with fear, edged closer to Mordruin.

"You would kiss the Skaveen blade? And serve our mistress?" he asked them.

Both blinked away tears, but resolutely nodded. Mordruin turned to Scallifor. "Let us take them."

The two Skaveen held out their steel to the pirates, each of whom kissed a blade then winced as they felt it plunge into their vitals.

Without further hesitation, Mordruin and Scallifor leapt aboard the *Scavenger* and it rose as easily as it had coasted down. On its decks, slumped by the rail, two forms were already stirring, two new servants for the Navigator's bizarre crew.

Below the sleek vessel, in the chaos of night and sea, the flailing tendrils of Crimson Island lashed impotently upwards. As they smashed back into the foaming seas, the warriors above could hear the final mad convulsions of the island mass and the *Sleekfin* as they folded into themselves and plunged down into the abyss that was the ocean's retribution.

THE END OF WISDOM

Gary Myers

In my youth, when the name of the sorcerer Eibon was little known to the world at large, I valued knowledge above all things and traveled far to acquire it. I sat at the feet of the great masters of wisdom wherever I could find them. I also sat at the spiritual feet of the greater masters whom I could not find, who had departed the earth long centuries before, but whose lore lived on in books of papyrus and parchment. I traveled to the great seats of civilized learning, to Uzuldaroum, Cerngoth and Oggon-Zhai. And not only to these, but also to the wild waste places that lie between, where the voices of devils are more clearly heard and the sleep of the gods is lighter. But the greatest journey I ever made was not to consult with devils or gods, or to study under masters living or dead. For these are only the beginnings of wisdom, and my quest was for its end.

The end of wisdom? To some the concept will no doubt seem childish. How can wisdom have an end? It is, after all, a mere catalog of facts. It is a finite catalog of infinite facts. It is a ring that rolls outward from a pebble dropped in the center of a lake. The more knowledge grows within the ring, the more it touches ignorance without. So we are told and so we believe. Yet in our heart of hearts we know that true wisdom is something more. That as the ring of water on the lake must finally reach the shore, so wisdom itself must reach an end, a point at which the wise may stand and view the pattern of all existence as a single meaningful whole. So that when I heard of an ancient monastery where the end of wisdom was said to reside, I had to see it for myself.

But first I had to find the place, and that would not be easy when my authorities themselves were in contention. The only thing they agreed upon was in putting the monastery at the southern end of the Eiglophian Mountains, which is as much as to say the southern end of the Hyperborean continent itself. The journey would be long and hard for one starting, as I was, at the northern end. It would also be fraught with peril from the cruel beasts and crueler men that lurk in the jungles that lie between. But I would be safe from their depredations, secure under the protection of a most effective army: my little family of domesticated Voormis, the huge and hairy ape-things that accompanied me in my travels.

These Voormis are worth a story in themselves. I acquired them in the course of one of my earliest journeys, on the heights of Mount Voormithadreth, the mountain that bears their name. A band of hunters had discovered a nest of a dozen Voormi young while returning from the expedition that had killed their sire and dam. Rather than kill the young ones also, they decided to preserve them for a more spectacular demise in the arena of Uzuldaroum. I convinced these hunters that my ready coin was harder and brighter than the visionary gold of the city folk, and so attached the little monsters to myself. I did it as a mere caprice, but my new pets were incapable of making such distinctions. They repaid my small kindness with a fierce and protective loyalty, a loyalty which, when later joined to the fearless strength and ferocious cunning of Voormi maturity, gave me a personal bodyguard such as even the most desperate robber band would go out of its way to avoid.

Yet the very maturity that created my bodyguard also doomed it to destruction. It was bad enough when one or another of the young males rose to challenge me for primacy in the pack. But when the females, who were even more repellent than the males, began to gaze upon my person with lust-filled eyes, I had no recourse but to terminate our association. But when I set out to find the end of wisdom this termination was still a year or two in the future.

We marched along the eastern side of the Eiglophian range, in the green shade of the adjacent jungle, which beats against its impassive base like waves against a rocky shore. My Voormis, being themselves creatures of the mountains, would perhaps have preferred the higher ground. But the jungle offered better shelter from the watchful eyes of potential enemies, as well as a more reliable source of water and game. Our sustenance depended wholly on what we could find and kill, since our journey was too long for us to carry provisions with us. And there were no settlers along the way from whom to acquire them through honest or dishonest means. There were no signs of human habitation anywhere.

For all the evidence I could see to the contrary, I might be the only man to have come to this place since either was created. It made me wonder whether my authorities had any factual basis for their claims, or whether they were sending me to the ends of the earth for nothing.

And then, early one morning about a month into our trek, our path was crossed by a road. I use the term loosely, for it was really just another path marked out by two parallel rows of small white stones. It was such a path as might be found in many a modest garden. Except that the path in the garden would have been straight and well tended, while this one was broken and half erased by the unchecked luxuriance of the jungle. Still, even the most neglected path suggests the nearness of civilization. And since there was only one civilized spot known to me in all this desolate region, and that the object of my search, I decided that the path was too important a clue not to be followed at once. Yet my Voormis were hardly the traveling companions to help me win the confidence of those I hoped to encounter at the end. So I left them to their own devices and proceeded by myself.

The path became more promising the longer I followed it. Its appearance changed little on the level land, but as the ground began to climb toward the feet of the looming mountains, its condition improved markedly. Maybe this was because the destroying jungle found it more difficult to get a purchase in the rockier soil. But in places the jungle seemed to have been driven back from the path in an effort to preserve it. Yet this was nothing to what I found a few yards further on. Here the jungle thinned enough to form a sort of clearing, and in the midst of this clearing was a little group of artificial structures, the first such I had seen in weeks. They were not very sophisticated structures. They were little more than rustic cottages, with walls of palm fronds woven together across frames of tree boles lashed with vines, and with roofs of more palm fronds laid down as a thatch. Yet their very impermanence seemed to show that there were men here to maintain them. And a moment later the man himself arose in their midst to confront me.

This man was one of the strangest figures I have ever seen. He was easily one of the oldest. He wore a long robe of simple white, and his white beard and hair fell over his breast and shoulders like a stole. But it was not in his age that the strangeness lay. It was not his clothing or his hair that made him seem so out of place in this setting so primitive and remote. The lowest aborigine could live as long or dress as well as he could. But the aborigine could never match his bearing. For although he dwelt in the depths of the wilderness, he bore himself with an air of civilized refinement that would not have been unsuited to the richest temple in Uzuldaroum.

"Pardon this intrusion," I said. "I am Eibon of Mhu Thulan. I have traveled long from that distant land to find this monastery and learn the wisdom it has to impart. Kindly inform your abbot of my arrival."

But the old man did not move from his place.

"The abbot knows of your arrival already, Eibon. I have held that office for the past seven years, since my predecessor, Mnardian, was compelled by age to relin-quish it. I hold that office as I hold every office this monastery has to bestow, for the simple reason that there is none other left to fill it. My name is Ruelphagor."

I bowed deeply.

"I beg your pardon, Ruelphagor. If I failed to recognize your holiness at once, it is only because my long exile from human society has impaired my ability to discern it. It is over a month since I left my home in the far-off north, and it is nearly as long since I last looked my fellow man in the face."

"And what brings you to me from Mhu Thulan in the far-off north? What is your purpose in coming here?"

"No light one, you can be sure. I am by avocation a student, a philosopher, a seeker after hidden things. In the course of my studies I learned of a certain mon-astery here in the distant south, a monastery like no other in the width and breadth of the world. For where other monasteries may house one or two facets of the totality of wisdom, in this monastery alone resides the end of wisdom itself. I knew not whether this monastery was real, but as long as the possibility remained I had to try to seek it out. And now, after many days and many miles, my search has brought me to you. So tell me, Ruelphagor. Is this the place I have come so far to find?"

"Yes. This is the monastery where the end of wisdom resides."

"And will you now reward my search by telling me what the end of wisdom is?"

"No."

"No?"

"Do not misunderstand me, Eibon. I do not withhold it from you willfully. But the end of wisdom is not a thing that can be told. If that were so, then the knowledge would have spread across the world long ago, and you would have no need to seek it here. No. There are things in this life that can only be known through experiencing them. The end of wisdom is one of these."

"Then say no more. For who would be content with airy words when the reality behind them is within his grasp, when he himself stands on the threshold of truth? May I cross that threshold now?"

"Follow me."

With that he turned and started away between the huts of his rustic compound. I was prepared to follow as far as he might lead me, but I soon found that the compound had almost no depth at all. There were no more than four buildings in the whole impoverished place. But a few yards behind them a black cliff rose, a clear demarcation of where the jungle ended and the mountains began. At first I thought that this cliff was a purely natural formation. Then I saw that, whatever its original state, it had been so smoothed and polished by the hands of men that it more resembled an artificial wall. This resemblance was only helped by the fact that there was an opening in its lower face, a dark cave as rectangular as a door.

I have said that the cave was dark, but I soon saw that this was not the case. It merely seemed so in contrast to the relative lightness of the surrounding stone. In fact the cave was wide enough, and the sun low enough in the heavens, that the daylight shone inside the door nearly as brightly as on the doorstep. But if the daylight was bright inside the door, it quickly became less so as my guide led me behind it. For the passage continued as a shaft or tunnel straight back through the solid stone as far as the eye could see. And it showed numerous side passages along the way, affording brief glimpses of halls and galleries otherwise lost in the subterranean darkness. Clearly this was the real monastery, of which the rustic compound formed the merest dooryard. Yet for all the skill and toil it represented, the chief impression it made on me was of an animal's burrow: dark, cramped and utterly oppressive.

"You are troubled, Eibon?"

"Say rather, puzzled. Wisdom is too vast a thing to be confined in any space. How then can it be held within these narrow halls?"

"Your puzzle is easily solved. This monastery does not contain the end of wisdom in any literal sense. All that it really provides is a point of vantage, a place from which the vastness can be viewed and comprehended. All that it really offers is a vision of the truth."

"Yet not all visions are equally of value. They are only as solid as the foundations they rest upon. What is the basis of this one?"

"None can say for certain. Some have surmised that it is a purely physical phenomenon, the effect of a volcanic gas vented from caverns below. Others, that it is the magical device of a mighty sorcerer of old, who wished to leave for those who came after him a record of the lesson he had taken a lifetime to learn. Still others, that it is a spiritual sending direct from the gods themselves. On one thing only have all agreed. He who enters the chamber of vision, who opens his eyes to the sights it has to show, he indeed attains the end of wisdom."

The side passages were all behind us,

and the light dim and gray in the distance, when the main passage stopped us before a door. I recognized at once that it was no ordinary door. All the other doors had been open and unobstructed. This one was covered with a leather hanging. Past all the other doors my host had preceded me. Here he pulled the hanging aside and motioned for me to precede him. But before I could do so he raised a hand to stop me.

"Not so fast, Eibon. First I have a duty to perform, for my office forbids me to let you proceed without a word of warning. This is no show to indulge a foolish curiosity. It is the end of wisdom itself. You cannot see it and not be changed by it, and perhaps in ways you cannot imagine. If you turn back, you will have wasted a long journey, and you will wonder to the end of your days what would have happened if you had not. But if you go forward, you will never wonder or doubt again. Now is the time to choose."

"My choice was made before you offered it. I will go forward."

I did so, and the hanging fell closed behind me.

The room in which I found myself was more like a tomb than a repository of wisdom. It was as small and confining as a tomb, and as somber as death with its walls of black obsidian. But it was not as well furnished as many tombs, for all it contained was a low dais of three stone steps and a high-backed stone chair rising like a throne from the center. The chair faced away from the only door. There was no daylight here. There was, however, a kind of vaporous glow hanging in the air above the dais, enfolding the chair in a cloud of hazy light. The room seemed an unlikely place in which to look for wisdom. But if I had learned nothing else in my young life, I had learned that wisdom may sometimes be found in the unlikeliest of places. I mounted the dais, sat down on the chair and waited for whatever the room had to show me.

At first it seemed to have nothing to show, nothing but black obsidian walls on every side of me. But presently it occurred to me that the walls themselves might be the medium in which the vision would appear. The walls behind and to either side were too pitted and scarred with the marks of their cutting to make that very probable. But the wall before me, while still somewhat rough at the outer edges, was in the center polished as smooth as window glass. It might have been window glass indeed for there was a second chamber visible behind it. My view of this chamber was somewhat murky, like the view of something drowned in muddy water. But it could not hide the fact that the chamber was lit and appointed like my own with a second dais, a second chair and a second man sitting upon it. Neither could it hide the fact that the second man was myself.

I regarded my reflection with all the interest of a man who could find nothing better to amuse him. Yet the study was not a disagreeable one. My figure was tall and lean, and dressed in a plain black suit of almost priestly austerity. My face was regular and pleasant, with a luminous brow, dark eyes and a neatly trimmed black beard. My expression, though, was reserved and skeptical, as of one who suspects a cheat and is determined not to be taken in. My expression might well be skeptical. For while no one would seriously refute the idea that knowledge of self is a worthy end of wisdom, and one of the most difficult to attain, yet the idea is neither so difficult nor so obscure as to require a great journey to arrive at it. I hated to think that I had come all this way to find only an uncommon looking-glass.

But suddenly the expression changed. The dark eyes lost their luster. The white face grew blank and smooth as virgin parchment. The firm mouth slackened and fell slightly open in the characteristic expression of an idiot. What did this mean? Surely my own face bore no such look. Then what purpose could the mirror have in showing this look upon it? Perhaps it was to illustrate another idea, the idea that even the most learned man is but an ignoramus when measured against the scale of what he does not know. Yet this new moral was no more satisfying than the first one had been. And it was even less satisfying when, a moment later, two enormous blowflies appeared from nowhere to light well apart on the blank white face, and to crawl toward each other in zigzag paths that slowly converged on one of the staring eyes.

There was no mistaking the reflection then, or the moral to which it pointed. But if this were all the mirror had to teach, the lesson would be over. And the mirror's revelations had barely begun. Now the face was covered with flies, covered so completely that only the eyes looked out. They looked like eyes in a featureless mask: not living eyes in a dead mask, but dead eyes in a living one. For the eyes were fixed and motionless, but the mask was never still. It crept and crawled in the hazy light with the restless

black bodies that composed it. It shifted and shone with their reflective wings, shifted and shone for all the world like a veil of polished sequins.

Nor did the revelations end there. The mask of flies had dispersed and departed, leaving in its place a second mask composed of small white worms. The worms were even more restless than the flies had been. They twisted and twined endlessly over and under and around each other, weaving themselves into a veritable fabric of wriggling, writhing life. But they were also less stable than the flies. Their living fabric frequently ruptured to show glimpses of the dead one beneath. And they constantly crowded each other from the ravaged face to rain down upon the black-sheathed belly below, the belly which had grown big and round through the action of internal fermentation.

I describe these sights with considerably more calm than I felt in seeing them. I had witnessed worse things in my pursuit of wisdom without undue distress. Yet the detachment we feel in contemplating distant ills is harder to preserve in the face of more immediate ones. We may watch the destruction of a perfect stranger and never turn a hair, yet the destruction of a friend or dear one cannot but inspire us with horror. And who is dearer to Eibon than Eibon? I felt the cold tickle of every worm that crept across my reflected face. I felt my stomach churn within me as my reflected stomach bloated, as it blew up like a pig's bladder inflated to amuse a child.

The latter in particular held my horrified attention. It continued to swell within the constraining clothing until one by one the overstrained fastenings broke. Then it went on swelling without constraint. But it could no more contain the pressures of its swelling than the clothing could contain the belly itself. And finally the inevitable happened. Like an inflated bladder pricked by a pin, it burst asunder with a loud and loathsome pop.

There are limits to what a man can endure even the pursuit of wisdom, and I had now reached mine. Throwing my arms across my eyes, I leaped to my feet and staggered down the dais steps to where I knew the door should be. I plunged headlong through the leather hanging into the outer passage, to fall facedown on the hard stone floor at the feet of the waiting Ruelphagor.

"You impress me, Eibon," the old monk said in a tone of genuine admiration. "Of the many wise ones who have preceded you on your quest, few have stayed to face its end for as long as you have done. And of those few, not one has walked away on his own two feet instead of being dragged out by his heels. You must be possessed of an unusually strong vitality, or under the protection of a very powerful god, to have survived the ordeal in any shape. Yet no vitality is strong enough, and few gods powerful enough, to have shielded you from its ill effects completely."

What was the old man talking about? The only ill effect I felt was a temporary nervous weakness, the natural result of my having subjected myself to a severe mental strain. Yet the ordeal must have tapped my physical as well as mental strength for, when I tried to raise myself to my feet, I only succeeded in lifting my head a foot above the floor. When I opened my mouth to speak, I was unable

to give utterance to anything more coherent than a gurgling moan. And an instant later I could not do even that, because a rain of small white worms had fallen from my jaws to writhe and wriggle on the stone flags inches below my face.

"Do not speak," Ruelphagor advised. "Too little breath remains to you to spend it in pointless conversation. And there is nothing you can say to me that I have not already heard. Yet be consoled. These effects, I believe, will pass with time. And even if they will not, you can take some comfort in knowing that, of all the wise who remain in the world, you are one of the very few who have nothing left to learn. But that is for the future. For the present, I regret that I must withdraw from you the hospitality of this monastery. Your company is no longer as pleasing as it was, and your odor is offensive. Follow me."

There was no answer to make to this, even if I had been capable of making it. There was nothing to do but drag myself to my nerveless feet and shuffle after my erstwhile host on stiff and awkward legs. There was nothing to do but suffer my expulsion from the stifling darkness of the ancient monastery to the fresh green shade of the jungle.

The rest of my story is quickly told. Ruelphagor was correct in his surmise that the effect would pass with time. At the end of three days I observed a slight improvement in my condition, in the form of a softening of the sinews and a loosening of the limbs. At the end of three months I could walk among my fellow men without instilling them with terror. At the end of six I could regard myself in a mirror without disgust.

But I foresaw none of this on the

evening I stumbled down the jungle path to the camp where my Voormis waited. Then it was all I could do to muster sufficient control of my throat and tongue to croak a simple order. Maybe I was wrong to do it. Maybe all sources of knowledge are equally sacred, and equally to be valued above any number of human lives. But I was young and intemperate, and the events of the day had not inclined me to be otherwise. Nor can I be certain, even now, that I regret very deeply the order I gave to my brutal servants. The order to show the ancient monk my own idea of the end of wisdom. The order to twist off his venerable head and burn his monastery to the ground.

YELLOW SHADOWS

Steffan Aletti

The King: *I stand before you under Carcosa's two moons, a shadow to my right, another shadow to my left. We are in a land of shadows. They are the gift of our two moons. I stand between the shadows, do I not? Or do I? Are you quite positive which of us is shadow and which is not? Perhaps we are all three shadows? Perhaps none of us is a shadow. The world of two moons is different from yours. My friend, I will confide in you. I am always the substance. It is* you *who are the shadow.*
—King in Yellow, *Act. 2, scene 4*

"A child can have only one fantasy, and that is power." The Marquis toyed absentmindedly with the ponytail of his peruque as he spoke. He plucked at the stiff strands of the carefully arranged hair at the back of his neck. Grains of powder glittered like diamonds as they tumbled off his wig and scattered in and out of the shafts of sunlight aimed by the stained glass window behind him.

The Marquise, her face dwarfed by the enormous foot-high coiffeur M. Léonard had just taken five hours to create, ignored him. Indeed, it seemed as if the Marquis was barely listening to himself as he absentmindedly toyed with the gold fob dangling from the deep pocket of his brocade vest. "That is the one thing that is missing from a child's world. Power. A child has no interest in sex. A *favoured* child like our Jean lacks no comforts or amusements. What he lacks is control—yes, he has some over his servants, but he has no control over his parents or his tutors. Put simply, he has no control over his life. He must do what everyone tells him to do. That is probably why he has created this ridiculous world over which he can play despot."

"What do these musings have to do with anything," his wife the Marquise muttered testily. "Our son refuses to get out of bed. He refuses to study. He refuses to attend Court with us today. He should be cultivating his manners, at his age he should be eyeing young ladies and following our lead through the intricacies of court etiquette and politics."

She stood abruptly. The shifting of the voluminous folds of her striped Polonaise gown sounded like distant waves pawing a sandy beach. "Why he should be *affianced* by now, but hardly anyone knows him. Prospective families considering beneficial alliances are looking forward to meeting him, and he is nowhere to be seen. He is in his room playing at his fantasies."

"It hardly matters. We will have no difficulty whatsoever in attaching him to a good and preferably wealthy family."

"Yes, but what kind of family? I will not give a . . . a . . . a *grocer's* daughter our name just because her father is wealthy. Jean must marry *above* our station not below it."

"There *aren't* that many families above our station," the Marquis snuffed. "You condemn our son to a very small universe of choice."

"Well, those that *are* above our station are being put off by word that something isn't quite right with the boy," she went on, ignoring her husband's elitist pique. "We must get Jean out of the house and into society. We must cleanse his mind of this unwholesome darkness and these frightening fantasies of his and set him about the business of . . . of . . . well . . . of *life*."

II

Jean had little interest in *life* as his parents knew it. He was unconcerned with the court and its politics or its intricate etiquette. Fancy dress bored him, as did the Court's general amusements— balls, banquets, musical extravaganzas, religious ceremonies and hunts. It was all an enormous and exhausting waste of time, so far as he was concerned. He was happiest at home, in his rooms, studying his precious manuscript.

Jean was dark-haired, with piercing eyes as big and dark as Spanish olives. His complexion, no doubt owing the fact that he rarely left his rooms, was sallow, his skin waxy and punctuated by a few rough, reddish patches which at least added some tint to an otherwise colourless and almost translucent skin. He was small in stature and extremely thin, built far more like his father, who had a tidy, compact body, than his large-framed and puddingy mother.

As a child, Jean was left largely to his own devices and the care of servants who were happy enough to ignore him so long as he caused no mischief. A curious boy, used to finding amusements on his own, he would explore the seemingly endless storage rooms at his family's various chateaux while his parents were off at court or tagging along with the king and queen on their endless royal progresses.

He investigated room after room, his footsteps echoing against the immense silence of mammoth, high-ceilinged chambers. He would run his hands over cold, smooth marble tabletops, inspect the complexities of centuries-old marquetry, or examine the brushworks on paintings that he indifferently took for wall decoration, but that future generations would declare masterpieces (in fact, Jean generally found the intricately-carved and brilliantly-gilded frames rather more entertaining than the paintings they held). In enormous storage rooms he opened trunks filled with musty clothes, wormy velvets punctuated by balding ermine, or shimmering silks that would sometimes collapse into motes of dust as he held them in his hands. He tried on pieces of armour— greaves, gauntlets, cuirasses—and, pretending he was Roland or the Duke of Parma, banged heavy swords and halberds against ancient shields and helmets. It would no doubt disappoint the future curators and patrons of some of the world's great museums to learn that the dents still visible in some of the most prized items in their armour collections were put there not in the heat of combat by a desperate warrior on some forgotten rampart, but by a bored child amusing himself on a rainy afternoon.

These great halls and abandoned storage rooms eventually became Jean's favourite playgrounds, the only places in a life strictly bound by convention and caste where he could indulge his imagination. These jumbled clothes, documents, silver and plate were his family's history - the chronicle of a great and noble house, a dynasty not so great in the exercise of arms and power as in the practice of political perspicacity and rapaciousness. The genius of generation after generation of Fleurys was the canny understanding that a life lived slightly more at the edge than at the center of great events was a richer and possibly longer life. Thus Jean's ancestors accumulated rather than dispensed, appropriated rather than bestowed, subverted rather than conquered and, in the end, bequeathed only what was necessary – and only in the face of death.

Gradually, as Jean made his musty way through his childhood and into adolescence, he began to find more interest in manuscripts. As was typical of the age, the family entrusted most of its written records to local monasteries, but the Fleury family was noted for one of the great private libraries of France. It contained over a thousand books at a time when a hundred books made up a formidable library indeed. While Jean found the archaic language and crabbed script of rare medieval manuscripts hard going, he did enjoy reading material from the recent past—anything within the past 100 years. He found Rabelais baffling, but laughed heartily at Moliere; he was bored to distraction by Guillaume de Lorris and the Roman de la Rose, but gloried in the brittle poetry of Racine.

Not everyone can point to the moment when his or her life changes, or the very thing that changes it; but Jean could. He could tell you to the second, he could describe the very *moment* it happened. In fact, he frequently did—to his bored parents, to distracted servants, to other young people at Court. It was an epiphany, and his insistence on recounting it and dwelling on it was the foundation of the general rumour that the boy was not quite right.

It was a dark, rainy early spring day, March 18. His parents were, not surprisingly, away. It was after a modest lunch that he climbed the rickety library ladder in his family's Beauvais palace to the very highest shelf to inspect an area that, judging by the rich layers of dust that lay almost like wool over everything, had been untouched for decades. It appeared to contain largely legal documents, but behind the bound copies of chronicles, contracts, deeds and wills lay a casket fashioned of an odd, lightweight, opaque material wearing a formidable, rusted lock. It was carved with obviously old but extremely odd figures. He examined the box, scrutinizing what looked like naked women kneeling before monstrous figures with misshapen faces and distorted bodies. A young man now, Jean's interest was piqued by the naked women. Though he regularly walked through corridors and sat in rooms with enormous paintings of naked goddesses lurching through the air dragging great, dimpled buttocks and massive breasts, he found himself excited by these small, odd carvings of more humanly-scaled women in apparent supplication. Unable to spring the rusted lock, he took the box back to his rooms at the end of the day.

Jean normally dreamt in shades of grey, but this night he dreamt of a great yellow hall so bright that his mind's eye ached, a court filled with bizarrely dressed figures. He saw a beautiful woman on her knees, completely naked before a huge, masculine figure wrapped entirely in vivid, wormy yellow silks and wearing a repulsive mask. He saw another figure come up behind her and slip a rope around her neck and begin to strangle her. She pulled desperately at the rope, her face turning red, her eyes bulging, her tongue protruding as she grunted and gasped. The great figure in yellow laughed and put his arm around Jean's shoulder as they watched the woman's death throes. Jean awoke in a sweat, to find he had experienced his first sexual climax.

The very next morning, he used the breakfast utensils to pry open the lock on the strange box. Inside the small gilded chest, wrapped in moldy cloth of gold, was a manuscript—perhaps some 80 pages of crabbed handwriting from a much earlier age. Jean carelessly unrolled the first set of pages. There was a handwritten note in the upper left margin: "Drame de Jean Marescot." Beyond that, nothing was intelligible. At the top of the page, in large letters, were the words "Xj Jdr jb Tbpzj." It appeared to be a title, but what could it mean? Further down on the page, the first word of the main body of the manuscript was "Fbllrhb." Page after page of similar gibberish followed.

Jean was baffled but intrigued. He equated the box with the dream he had had the previous night, the dream that had introduced him to an unimagined world of strange and intense—if morbid—sexuality. The manuscript almost certainly held the key to more of that world. It all *had* to mean something. After all, Jean surmised, *nobody* would take the time to write so many pages of nonsense.

III

Michel Marescot, a physician, scholar and occultist, is best known to narrow circles as the writer and publisher of pamphlets and broadsides about witchcraft and demonology sometime around 1600. He was considered most learned and pious, having taken some minor holy orders, and he died during one of the 17th century's fairly regular visits from the plague. And there is one reference to him as "Michel le bossu," which suggests he might have been a hunchback or otherwise physically misshapen, though it should be remembered that in those days deformity was equated with evil, and unpopular people were frequently referred to and even pictured as misshapen in an attempt to characterize them symbolically. There is no evidence of Marescot's physical appearance one way or another.

What *is* known, however, is that towards the end of his life, Marescot was attached to the great Fleury household as a physician and personal confessor to Madame la Marquise herself. In addition to his medical and priestly duties, he tended to the family's great library at Orleans, and regularly amused his master and mistress with works of poetry and the occasional drama, virtually all now lost. According to family legend chronicled by a later servant, Marescot, the Marquise herself and six or seven (accounts differ) of the household servants were struck by disease during the actual enactment of a play, an apparently scandalous work of mysterious and dark provenance. Beyond this tantalizing suggestion, the chronicler limits himself to the implication that the disease was a form of divine retribution for taking part in or tampering with something best left alone. "The pestilence apparently struck with such incredible rapidity," says the anonymous writer, that "the Marquise did not have time to dress or leave the stage before she was covered with pustules that burst as her body darkened and bloated." Surely the chronicler meant to write that she did not have time to *undress.*

Of course, at that time, it was hardly uncommon for the plague to visit multiple deaths on a household, or for that matter to wipe out entire families. Nor was it uncommon for chroniclers, who were generally monks or religious scribes, to attribute any scourge to God's vengeance for some trespass against the Church.

But Jean knew nothing of this matter; the chronicle would lay undisturbed and unread in the nearby Fleury Abbey for another century and a half before being identified and translated by scholars into modern French.

The work's general construction was very visible: a short word, a colon, a line or lines, a space and another short word, colon and more lines. A religious service with responses? The physical structure was very similar to that of many pages in Jean's missal. Or perhaps a drama. Any page from Moliere had the same general look. Structure aside, the work's first word, the baffling "Fbllrhb," followed by a colon and the equally meaningless "Bxdjl" was the beginning of a totally incomprehensible jumble of undecipherable letters.

Jean eagerly enquired as to what it all might mean, first of his parents, then others at court, then finally even the servants, whom he thought might be familiar with distant, barbaric languages. But nobody could fathom *Fbllrhb* or *Bxdjl*. No one knew of any languages that

would sustain unpronounceable constructions such as *FBL, BXD* or *KM*.

Jean could see words and patterns repeated: the puzzling *Fbllrhb,* almost always followed by a colon, frequently appeared at the beginning of a line, and references to *Xj Jdr* ran from the first page to the last.

Jean eventually realized it must be some sort of code, a device whereby the writer could hide his meaning to all but a select circle. But he had not the least idea as to how to go about deciphering it.

Of course cipher had been used for centuries by everyone from clandestine lovers to the king's spies and secret service, and Jean became eager for once to attend Court in the hopes of meeting somebody who might be able to give him some pointers in the art of decoding. In fact, after inquiries, he engaged the attention of a Baron Lescaux who, it was rumoured, had spied for the Crown during the recent unpleasantness with the Netherlands. Amused by the boy's insistence, the Baron, an enormous, noisy, obese man who gave lie to the superstition that successful spies are necessarily inconspicuous, graciously agreed to have a look at the manuscript. Jean eagerly turned his treasure over to Lescaux.

After only a few days, the Baron returned the manuscript to Jean with a curt note:

"A simple code. Add the value of one to the first letter, add two to the second, three to the third and so on progressively until the alphabet is exhausted. Thus: A=B. B=D. C=F and so on until 13 letters are added to M, so it becomes Z. Then you start over, adding 14 letters to N so it becomes B. Continuing, O=D, P=F, until finally to Z, 26 is added to become—or, more accurately—to *remain* Z. I have read some distance into the manuscript. It is a play, a pretty one, so I first thought. I have arrived at the second Act and can—or will—not read more. Burn it, my boy and attend pursuits more appropriate to your age and station."

Ignoring the Baron's unwanted advice, Jean immediately applied the decoding scheme. How incredibly simple, he thought. *Xj Jdr jb Tbpzj* is transliterated to *Le Roi en Jaune*, or *The King in Yellow*. *Fbllrhb* is *Cassilda*, apparently the name of a female character. *Bxdjl*, the first spoken word, is nothing but *Alors* which would loosely be translated as "Well, then."

Jean immediately applied the scheme and began the extraordinarily laborious task of translating what he now knew to be a play. His parents, briefly buoyed by hopes that the boy's sudden interest in attending Court signaled a change for the better in his personality, were bitterly disappointed to find him now even more reclusive, spending day and night in his rooms, counting the alphabet on his fingers as he brought the long-hidden play out of the darkness of centuries letter by letter.

Perhaps it should be asked here, how and why this ancient, mouldering manuscript could so catch the fancy of a young man who should normally have been out riding and hunting and hawking. Why did he turn himself inward to sit day after day cocooned in his expansive rooms poring over its ancient, crabbed script for the mysteries he believed so devoutly were therein to be found? What, conversely was it about this strange work that seemed invariably to find just such young men and women?

The work, like an opportunistic virus hunting a physically weak host, seemed through the centuries to seek out the im-pressionable, the unfocused or the unbalanced, the weak, the disenfranchised. One can trace its progress, sputtering like a fuse through centuries and across continents, appearing in different disguises—Greek, Latin, Chinese, Middle English, medieval Italian, Renaissance French, 18th Century German, late 19th century American English etc.—invariably leaving in its wake exploded lives and operatic tragedies. Threading its way through the milennia like a graveworm through a corpse, *The King in Yellow* seemed—and seems—always to find precisely the readers it needs to work its destructive enchantment. It and they have invariably been a match made, truly, in hell.

But such a study, clearly outside the scope of this highly-focused historical narrative, would perhaps be more within the realm of the forensic psychologist.

IV

Tired of studying, of trying to pierce the deep secrets and hidden philosophies so bafflingly encrypted by the careful Marescot, he called for a maid. Within moments, a small blonde girl wearing a mobcap appeared.

"Master?" she said, curtseying deeply.

"I wish to sleep now," he said, not looking up at her. "Prepare my room."

She busied herself snuffing the candles at the opposite end of the room. The bold horizontal stripes of her short saque backed jacket looked like rib bones, giving her an oddly skeletal look above her petticoat and aprons.

Suddenly Jean heard what sounded like strange, distant music.

The maid walked back from the far end of the room and began drawing the drapes near his bed.

"Wait," he cried. "Do you hear that music?"

She spun around startled and probably a little frightened. Jean was known to have a nasty temper, and was not liked by the servants. "No, Master," she whispered uneasily. "I hear nothing."

"You mean to say you cannot hear *anything*?" Jean was incredulous.

"Nothing, sir."

Jean threw his covers aside and, wearing only his nightshirt, leapt from his bed. He bounded over to the servant girl, grabbed her by the shoulders and shook her. "Nothing?" he shouted. With one hand he reached over and drew the curtain aside. An incredible radiance, pure golden yellow, flooded the room.

"I don't suppose you see that brilliant light, either?" he cried.

"I hear nothing, Sir. I see nothing, Sir. It is dark outside. Please, let me go. You're hurting me . . ."

Still holding her tightly, Jean looked out the window. Incredibly, instead of the usual manicured gardens punctuated by trees *in espalier*, his windows looked out on what appeared to be an enormous ballroom. It was a costume ball, just the sort of gala event Jean would have hated at Court, except here everything seemed unearthly and magical, freighted with deep significance, every movement conforming to some mysterious and profound choreography whose meaning as yet Jean could only guess at.

The ballroom was nearly blinding. Draperies, walls, columns, everything was done in the most vivid and explosive chrome yellow. Jean flung open the window and stepped out into the evening air. He seemed to float down to the ballroom floor. When he alighted, he found he was no longer nearly naked; instead he wore strange brilliant robes of a mysterious, glittering yellow cloth. At the corner of the giant room was a small musical group—a soft consort of strings and light reeded wind instruments. The melody, with its diapason-like accompaniment, had a distant, hollow and distinctly chilling sound with an unusual modality, something like a mixolydian mode except that in addition to the flat seventh, some tones—for instance the second and the sharp fourth—seemed totally absent.

He walked by the musicians, who were playing from memory. They looked out into the ballroom from their perch, a window balcony about five feet above the ballroom floor. They stared out into the lofty space, seemingly seeing nothing. He stood directly below, staring up at one of the violinists, but he could not engage his attention.

He turned to look at the dancers. They were paired—male and female Jean presumed, though with the odd, bulky costumes and masks it was impossible to tell. They held hands at arm's length and proceeded through a stately and complex choreography of turning and bowing. Beyond the mysterious dancing figures, Jean gradually made out an enormous throne made of a glowing, pulsing, translucent yellow material, perhaps amber. Seated on it was a large, powerfully-built masked figure wrapped in golden robes. Yellow gloves covered his immense hands, and a strangely-configured crown set with brilliant yellow garnets sat low on his brow.

Jean fell to his knees, terror gnawing at the pit of his stomach. *It was the King in Yellow himself, the Living God.* He *did* exist. Carcosa *existed.* It *was* all true.

Suddenly, the dancers stopped and turned to face a hooded figure entering the ballroom. She seemed very young, certainly no more than 15 or 16, and slight of build. A few golden blond curls tumbled from beneath a large, pointed hood, and bare toes appeared rhythmically from beneath the floor-length cloak as she walked slowly, rather numbly, to the center of the marble floor. There, she stood inside an inlaid circle of opalescent blue marble—the only spot in the entire room that wasn't a vivid yellow.

The King rose from his throne and made his way towards her as the couples parted to let him pass. He towered over her as he pushed the golden cloak from her shoulders. Jean drew in his breath sharply; he knew that she would be naked under the cloak, which fell in a puddle of shimmering almost liquid material at her bare feet.

She stepped out of it and kneeled in front of the King, raising her arms to him. Her small breasts fluttered like plump drops of water hanging from the lip of a garden pump, their nipples drawing themselves into hard, sharp buds. She closed her eyes and began to sway slightly to the rhythm of the music. The King turned away from her and began to look about the ballroom, his eyes glaring a shocking red behind his brilliantly yellow mask, his great chest and massive shoulders flexing behind his tight, bright yellow tunic. Slowly, he began to move about the room, ap-proaching one couple after another. Each pair in turn fell to its knees and raised their arms to him; he looked at them for a few moments, but always turned away.

Jean stood frozen, barely able to breathe. The room was now so bright it hurt his eyes but he dared not shield his face for fear of offending the King in Yellow. His head throbbed painfully in tandem with the infernal music, in tandem with his heart, which seemed about to explode from his chest.

He knew the King would come to him. He held his breath and tried to be so still as to be invisible, but he felt it like a chill in his bowels: the King would come to him and he would be called on to perform some act to prove his worthiness.

The King was at the farthest end of the ballroom, his head towering above the groveling courtiers, but nearly lost in the flood of brilliant yellow that now seemed to oscillate and reverberate with the deafening music.

And here was the moment. He felt it. The King turned. The courtiers all disappeared in a blinding yellow explosion. Only the King was there, way way down at the end of the Hall, which seemed now five times its original length. The King, a tiny figure seen through the wrong end of a telescope, blindingly bright, fixed his scarlet eyes on Jean and began to approach. Everything seemed now to be in slow motion, like a terrifying underwater ballet. It seemed hours before the King arrived before Jean.

He stared at Jean, his red eyes glaring behind the ill-favoured mask. "You have found your way, my friend, into the shadows between the worlds of the living and dead," he said. "You straddle that heartbeat between life and death. It is the rare living being who enters our sphere; know that it is rarer still to leave. Have you the strength to remain with us?"

He handed Jean a brilliantly yellow, tasseled silk ribbon, thin as gold foil. Instinctively, Jean knew what to do with it. He must demonstrate his love for the King in Yellow, his absolute and unquestioning devotion.

He stepped behind the young girl, deftly snapped the thin cord into the air over the girl's head, looped it around her neck and pulled it tight. Her eyes bulged wide and her tongue pushed its way out of her mouth. Incredibly, the girl's arms remained raised in homage to the King. Jean struggled with the cord, pulling it tighter with all the strength he could summon. It bit deeply into her neck, disappearing altogether into the swelling, bruised flesh of her throat. Gradually, she closed her swollen eyes and relaxed her sweet features. She released a stream of urine that ran down her thighs and puddled at her knees. Her arms descended to her side as her head fell on her shoulder, as if she were napping. Breathless with the exertion of wrenching the life out of a human being, Jean relaxed his grip on the cord, which remained embedded deeply in her neck. The young blonde girl slid to the floor and seemed to fold herself into a limp ball.

The King put his hand on Jean's shoulder, a gesture of camaraderie. "She dies every night, a slow, agonizing death that is in no way diminished or softened by its familiarity," the King said in a distant, rusty voice. "Every day she is resurrected and freshly fleshed to become the soft, nubile and desirable young virgin she was so long ago—*how* long ago

you cannot imagine. That is at once Cassilda's burden and her glory. For Cassilda, death, life and love conjunct every night. She has had a thousand deaths and a thousand lovers, and will continue to do so forever.

"Cassilda is the perfect counterfeit of life. She sees, she even breathes—if only for a few hours—during which she lies, spread-eagled, between my world and yours, a simulacrum of life: she is no longer dead, but the taste of the grave never leaves her mouth. When she has consummated the act of love with the living, and when she has accepted the fluids of the living that unite the quick and the dead in order to permit the physical world to continue on its mundane way, she again returns to my world, to endure willingly the burden of a living mind in a corrupt, putrefying body."

Jean reached down, picked up the girl and carried her like a doll, arms and legs swinging limply. He laid her on a gleaming gold divan. He slid down next to her, took her in his arms, and ran his fingers through her golden hair. He looked deeply into her eyes, so heavy-lidded and mysterious in death, and began to kiss her still-warm, dry lips. Her eyes suddenly opened wide but remained dull and opaque; she smiled, and through her grinning rictus he could see drying blood between her teeth. She slid her black, swollen tongue into his mouth before he could form a scream.

In another explosion of brilliant yellow radiance, Jean saw the entire ballroom, seemingly from somewhere high above. It seemed to shift its shape, distorting itself first into a circle, than evolving into an ellipse, which itself began to develop hard, straight edges before folding in on itself. Its walls pulsed with the music, now become an incomprehensible roar. The dancers or courtiers or whatever they were seemed now to be little more than bestial gelatinous shapes rutting in slime. At the center of it all, Jean could see himself lying on the cooling body of the blonde girl, who slowly locked him in between her legs and arms in a claustrophobic embrace.

The King in Yellow stood tall and proud, his arms spread over the loving couple in a mysterious blessing as Cassilda's cold loins milked Jean of his seed.

Slowly, mechanically, Cassilda rose to a sitting position. The King offered her his gloved hand and helped her to stand. He freed several strands of golden hair that were caught under the yellow cord. Jean rose, still panting.

"How little the living world understands," The King said to him. "Cassilda dies for your world every night; Cassilda rises for your world, like the sun, every day. Yet your world does neither her nor me any honour."

The King took her hand and gestured for Jean's hand. Cassilda stood and faced Jean, naked and unashamed as the King joined their hands.

"My husband," Cassilda said, her voice sounding strangely remote and foggy, her dead eyes partially shut and unfocused.

"My wife," Jean responded, uneasily.

The King approached the couple. From within his saffron robe, he pulled a mask similar to his and offered it to Jean, who took it it gratefully and fixed it to his face.

Cassilda pressed her naked body against him. He held her tightly as she began to dissolve in his arms. Her mouth fell open and her lips shriveled and peeled back, revealing numberless squirming maggots feeding on her bloated tongue. Her eyes began to bleach and wither into the depths of their sockets. Her nose shrank, creating the illusion that her nostrils were widening, and her breasts grew heavy and rolled like puddings down her chest. A foul sap began to leak from her shrunken eyes and nose and mouth and ears and from between her swelling, blackening legs. Jean recoiled, but Cassilda was cemented to him by the rancid juices now seeping from her every orifice as the outer layer of her skin began to blister and slither from her body; he pulled away from her grip, and the skin of her hand slid off the bone like a yellow kid glove. The bones of her hand, still partially covered in an unraveling network of pustulent veins and muscles, swiftly moved with an iron grip to pull her husband back into her decomposing embrace.

"You must not turn away," the King in Yellow shouted.

"Do not reject me, my husband," Cassilda wailed in a voice that sounded like falling sand.

Jean began to scream. Disentangling himself finally from the barely human shape made increasingly monstrous by putrefying gasses, purging liquids and infestations of humming insects, Jean began to run, at each step kicking or treading on rotting courtiers. He slipped and slid on a river of corruption directly into a gelatinous, roughly humanoid shape, whose surface was a mass of writhing larval life forms. The mask he had placed over his face now became a red-hot weight pressing against his cheeks and brow, filling his nostrils with the stench of his own searing skin. He writhed as he ran, stumbled and slid, shaking his head and tearing desperately at the mask, trying to get his fingernails under its edge to pry it off, but its seams had sunken into his flesh. He was indeed now one with the King in Yellow.

The light, which increased to an explosive frequency, suddenly disappeared and a monstrous blackness enveloped everything. Just before Jean gratefully relinquished his consciousness, he heard the King. "You wear my brand," he thundered, "but you have disappointed me and you have spurned Cassilda." The courtiers and Cassilda raised their voices to an accusatory howl as the King delivered a final malediction. "You will enjoy astonishing misfortune before we meet once more."

V

The girl, naked and twisted, the silk cord still biting deeply into her neck, lay on the floor at the side of his bed. Her face, which seemed to wear a petulant frown, was dark and congested, her once-limpid skin now mottled with purplish patches. Her eyes remained partially open, as if she were trying to sneak a look at the horrified servant who stood over her. Saliva leaked from her mouth.

"Oh my Lord," the servant gasped as he stared at the dead girl, "Master, what have you done?" He fell to his knees and lifted the girl, cradling her in his arms as he pushed the hair from her face. "Oh my Lord," he kept crying, "such a sweet girl. What have you done, Master? What have you done?" He began to cry, his hot tears falling on her upturned face and running down her cold cheek.

"What does it matter? I can do as I please. I *am* the King in Yellow now," Jean said, his eyes burning with imperious majesty and surprising *gravitas*, despite what appeared to be scabrous sores and fresh, suppurating scars covering his face. He lay in his bed, stretched out stiffly over satin sheets, which were, of course, yellow. "Remove her. She has served her purpose."

The servant picked her up and laid her gently on the foot of Jean's bed.

"Don't put that on my bed . . ." Jean began with indignation.

"I must cover her, Master," the servant said roughly. With an angry swipe of his arm he pulled the top layer of satin from Jean's bed and wrapped the girl in it, leaving only her head, her blonde hair and bare feet uncovered and dangling. He carried her tenderly from the room.

Within minutes all the servants knew what had happened. Within hours, so did the Marquis and Marquise.

"She is of no consequence," the Marquise said, waving her hand dismissively as her husband paced nervously. "Her parents are one of the scullery staff and the fourth *sous* chef. He is a disgusting creature, but he has a gift for meringue. They have both been compensated rather more graciously than necessary, and they will keep their silence." She sat with a crunching of silk and taffeta.

"You act as if this is all over with," the Marquis said nervously. "What if Jean attempts this sort of thing again? On somebody of consequence? On somebody in society?"

"Once he has arrived at his majority, he can do as he pleases," she said firmly. "What of the Duke de Montcréasse? Gossip says he satisfies his peculiar appetites by not only ravishing but also torturing his servants. Madame de Greliac insists she knows for a fact that for no reason beyond his amusement he has drowned several serving girls."

"First, Jean is not likely to become a duke. Second, we cannot trust him to await his majority to commit more of these acts. Moreover, for better or worse, we have arrived at a world where our rank no longer bestows upon us such immunity as we once enjoyed. I don't doubt that if there were substance to these rumours about Montcréasse, he would be brought down."

"What a shame," she sniffed. "My great, great grandfather said it when they executed DeRetz. 'Imagine,' he said, 'the world had become the kind of place where they can execute the Grand Marshal of France simply for . . . *sporting* with servant boys and girls. We have inherited a world where position and power mean nothing.'"

"Well, apparently he rather more than *sported* with them," the marquis grumbled, "he murdered dozens of them."

"But he was a *Grand Marshall*," she cried, shocked that such a high personage could even be criticized, let alone brought so low.

"I guess even then a Grand Marshal could go too far," the Marquis mused.

"That is just what my great, great grandfather meant," she huffed. "There was a time when a Grand Marshall would have been untouchable."

VI

The King nodded graciously at the Marquise de Fleury, his potato face a beaming mask of sweetly tempered condescension which darkened immediately as he turned back to the Marquis.

"Quite simply, Monsieur, he must be confined. You must convince your wife of this. There is no alternative."

"But Seigneur," the Marquis said with genuine pain in his voice, "surely keeping him at home would serve the same purpose while allowing him to be with those who care for him . . ."

"I'm afraid that cannot suffice. He cannot be trusted to those who care for him. Nature forbids you either to discipline him for his crimes or to provide the harsh treatments he must endure in order to be restored. *If* indeed he can ever be restored. Those who love him would necessarily be the very worst caretakers."

"But your Majesty, you consign my only son to a life of misery and punishment."

"I can do no less. We are no longer in the position we once were; we no longer rule the will of the people."

"The *people*," the Marquis said, stunned and baffled. "But what have they to do with *us*?"

"This discussion is over." The King turned away abruptly and began to converse with a charmingly pudgy woman with over-rouged nipples.

So Jean, in his favourite yellow silks decorated with powder blue ribbons, bound hand and foot and taken by sedan chair to a carriage waiting at the far gate. His parents, more mortified at this palpable insult to their honour and their class than desolate at the pain of separation, chose to be on holiday in the South.

There are no records at L'Hôpital St. Germaine to suggest what kind of treatment the young marquis received at the hands of his keepers. But enough is known of the contemporary attitude towards dangerous eccentricity to suggest that he was restrained, most likely starved, almost certainly beaten regularly, and probably subjected to ferocious poultices and emetics in an effort to purify and settle his mind.

Jean lived out his life at the Hôpital: seven more years of what was surely misery, until he was, according to the records, found with his throat slashed—which, it must be admitted, was not an uncommon death in this or any other madhouse at that time; the place must have been a hellish free-for-all in the days of the Directoire, as there was in effect no longer such governing body as there had been in the less egalitarian but somewhat more orderly days of the monarchy. The lowest echelon help was put in charge, and from various reports it was clear that restraints were applied haphazardly—some patients were chained, bound and gagged or beaten while others—though equally dangerous—had the run of the place. According to a number of extant first-hand accounts, more than a few visitors had to draw their swords to defend themselves from rampant lunatics.

Thus Jean avoided the guillotine to which his astounded and outraged parents were condemned within five years of his incarceration.

It was said the Marquis faced his end with diffidence if not equanimity, and as he was generally known to be a decent man despite his royal blood, and a soldier of some consequence during the Spanish difficulties of the previous generation, he was shown modest respect not only by *Monsieur de Paris*, but by the gen-erally unruly crowd.

Not so the Marquise, whose public utterances and actions had earned for her the contempt of the populace. The executioners dragged her up the 13 steps of the scaffold to watch at close quarters her husband's decapitation; then they forced her to her knees and held her while his dripping face was pressed against hers in a mocking, bloody kiss. Delighted, the crowd egged the scaffold crew on to offer them greater amusements. The Marquise, howling in horror and fury, her face dripping with her husband's blood, was up-ended and her great watery buttocks exhibited to the crowd, which roared in delight at the remarkably clear hand-prints the *sous* executioner left on each wobbling half-moon.

Monsieur de Paris, disinclined to go against the crowd's wishes but concerned with maintaining his reputation for pro-fessionalism and discipline, descended the scaffold and left the proceedings to his underlings. After about 20 minutes of humiliations that stopped just short of rape—no doubt owing less to the sensibil-ities of her tormentors than to the protec-tion afforded her by advanced age and flinty unattractiveness—she was kicked nearly naked over to the guillotine, dragged by a smart grip on her pudenda into the appropriate position on the *bascule*, strapped in, tilted horizontally and locked into the *lunette*. For the Marquise, the caress of Madame Guillo-tine was rough. By some trick of the posi-tion of her head or perhaps the angle at which her writhing body lay, the thun-dering blade caused her head to leap into the air through a shower of blood that splashed both executioners up to their waists though they had stepped away the usual distance and stood behind the wooden shield. And instead of dropping obediently into the waiting basket, Madame's head spun through the air and bounced three times before coming to rest at the edge of the platform. It was said that her naked buttocks persisted in quivering and spasming while the *sous* executioner pursued her rolling head, picked it up and said in a stage whisper "Still trying to get away, eh? That will not do, Madame la Marquise." The crowed roared its approval.

Unwilling as yet to relinquish the object of such amusement, several of the scaffold crew took a turn around the platform dragging the Marquise's headless corpse in their arms in an energetic *pas de deux* before turning it off the platform, limbs flying loosely as the headless trunk bounced down the 13 steps it had so recently ascended, to join a large wicker box from which a tangle of noble arms and legs protruded.

For more than a few days thereafter, all Paris giggled at a variety of jokes about Madame La Marquise de Fleury's "end."

VII

"Citizen, what will you do with all of this?" he gestured at the furniture, hangings, paintings, chests, service pieces and bric-a-brac piled none-too-carefully in the grand hall.

"I have invited dealers from every conceivable trade to pick through this mess," Frontenac replied. "I made it clear that I will take any offer short of outright theft in order to get rid of all of it, so I have no doubt that everything will disappear, most likely to end up in bourgeois homes at prices as outrageously high as they were purchased from us outrageously low."

"And the money thus generated?"

"Goes to the support of the widows and orphans of our gallant soldiers, of course" he said, bowing low.

"Good, good. When will the dealers arrive?"

"They begin to arrive today. I anticipate nearly everything cleared out by Friday."

And so it was. Dealers left with barely enough room to sit in carriages and coaches stacked high with canvasses signed by Watteau, Canaletto, Boucher and de Largilliere, tapestries from Beauvais and Aubusson, timepieces by Passement and Danthiou, watches by Breguet, enormous candelabras by Gouthière, furniture with inlay of rare mahoganies and amboyna wood and tulip by Riesener, porcelain from Sévres and Limoges, silverware by Paul de Lamerie, gold by Jean Bourguet etc. etc. Tons of manuscripts and lesser objects had already been burned or discarded as insufficiently valuable but still, so much remained that the immense Chateau was *not* emptied out by Friday; nor was it emptied out by the following Friday, nor yet the Friday after that.

In time, after visits from hundreds of grasping tradesmen, the great house was bled of its valuables; what little proved unsaleable was picked over by M. Frontenac himself, who took for himself a number of more modest items that combined value and portability; these included, for some reason he himself could not explain, a particularly ugly but clearly very ancient box of a mysterious yellowish material carved with a number of provocative if primitive figures.

As faithful to the *Directoire* as he had been to the Marquis and Marquise de Fleury, M. Frontenac kept meticulous accounts of every item—description, provenance where possible, value estimated, and the amount for which it was purchased and by whom. In fact, *doubly* conscientious as it were, M. Frontenac kept *two* meticulous accounts: the first, for the benefit of the *Directoire* and largely fictional, demonstrated clearly via receipts M. Frontenac's even-handedness and laudable honesty in amassing and turning over a fairly impressive sum to the widows and orphans fund. The other set of books was a far more accurate account of the same transactions, along with a completely *different* set of receipts to which were appended the details of a remarkable network of bribes and inspiredly underhanded dealings. This last set of books demonstrated that the sum paid out to the orphans and widows was in fact the *smallest* of the vast number of sums detailed in those books. The enormous profit—in gold, of course— would leave the country with M. Frontenac who, as an officer of the *Directoire*'s civil court, was not subject to search and seizure at the Swiss border. Thus did one of France's largest and oldest fortunes make its way out of the country.

But not before the old servant paid one last visit.

Much as he hated Jean, Frontenac was shocked at the "hospital" which had been Jean's home for nearly seven years. The odor of garbage and filthy flesh was so strong he nearly fainted as he was conducted through the dark, airless vestibule.

"The second floor, first door on the right," said a corpulent attendant with astonishing breath and a tricolour pinned to a stained and shiny lapel.

As Frontenac climbed, holding a perfumed handkerchief tightly to his nose and mouth and careful to avoid the excrement and rotted food splattered up and down the steps, a fat, naked woman with enormous, swaying breasts ran past him screaming something unintelligible. On the second floor landing, a few feet from Jean's door, a couple fornicated. Unable to look away despite his embarrassment, Frontenac was appalled to see the woman appeared unconscious—or perhaps even dead.

He knocked at the first door and entered, stepping over the woman's bare foot, which extended into the entrance to the room.

Old Frontenac wasn't sure he could endure another shock on this morning of shocks, but there, seated in the center of the room, poring over a well-worn manuscript, was a frail wreck of a man that bore an uneasy resemblance to the young Master. Unbelievable, thought Frontenac. It *was* Jean. The boy could hardly be 30, but he appeared ancient. His hair—what there was of it—was nearly white. The skin of his face consisted mostly of scar tissue, still red and angry after all these years; he was completely toothless; and his eyes, which barely had any life let alone awareness left in them, were deeply sunken and faded to a slate grey. Any viewer would have guessed the sexagenarian Frontenac to be the younger of the two.

Frontenac walked slowly over to the seated Jean. "You remember me, Master?" Jean did not look up.

"Oh, I remember *you*, sir, yes I do, yes I do," Frontenac said. He knelt and took Jean's hand in his, patting it. "Yes, Master, I will remember *you* to my dying day. If you do not recall me, perhaps you will do me the honour to recall my sweet Amelie, with her golden hair, her beautiful skin, her teeth, perfect as pearls. You remember *her*? She was one of your maids. She was 13, can you imagine that? Only 13. She was my daughter, my love child. I loved Jeanne, her mother—she worked in your kitchens, oh yes, only a scullery maid, but a beautiful, strong and, yes, even *noble* woman. She was married to that great fat Meilhac, one of the *sous* chefs, but she loathed him; and of course he was too busy eating to pay any attention to her. I'm *sure* you don't remember her or him. Perhaps you don't even remember me."

Frontenac looked squarely into Jean's eyes. There was no recognition. The old man shook his head sadly.

"You remember nothing, I see." He took a deep breath. "My time here is short, so let me refresh your memory quickly. You should, Master, remember my Amelie, because you *murdered* her. Oh yes, Master, you strangled her. I entered your rooms one morning to find you in your bed reading, while my darling daughter lay crumpled on the floor by your bed, a yellow silk ribbon biting into her swollen neck, her lips purple and her eyes red and staring, her little hands balled into fists, her sweet little breasts exposed, *my darling daughter* lay on the floor by your bed like *trash* to be taken out."

Frontenac's eyes were tearing as his voice rose in pitch and volume.

"You didn't even do Amelie the *courtesy* of paying attention as I gathered her poor, cold body in my arms and removed her, like last night's dinner tray, from your rooms. I had to notify Jeanne and

her husband of Amelie's death, and your mother gave me 25 francs to secure their silence. We and Père Gérôme and the garden staff buried Amelie that night at the edge of the family graveyard—it was an unmarked grave, but at least it was in hallowed ground.

"Jeanne collapsed and never really recovered; she died less than a year later. Meilhac drank up the 25 francs and remarried. But of course, *you* wouldn't pay any attention to such trifles, would you. *You* were too busy with your King in Yellow *merde* to care, weren't you."

At the name of his deity, Jean looked up at Frontenac. He weakly held up the manuscript in his lap and whispered "The King in Yellow, it's all here. "The secret is here. There is yet another cipher, another layer beyond the layer that I have translated. Alas," he said sadly, looking helplessly down into his lap, "the Baron is gone. Everyone is gone. There is no one left to help me discover it."

He looked back down at the paper. "I was once in the King's grace," Jean said emotionally, "but I did not have the fortitude to pursue the road His Majesty laid out for me, and I have suffered for my timidity."

He looked up at Frontenac with distant, rheumy eyes, tapping the manuscript in his lap. "But the secret is *still* here. I will find it and restore myself to grace."

"The secret is in *there*, is it Master?" Frontenac hissed. "No, I think the secret is *here* . . ." and he pulled out a small, very sharp knife. Jean stared at it briefly but didn't move or register any emotion. "Alas, Master, I came to exact my revenge on you for my darling daughter and my lovely mistress. Though I have neither the time nor the stomach to make *you* suffer the way you made *them* suffer, I *did* intend for you to feel some small percentage of their pain."

Frontenac turned and surveyed the filthy room. The ornate bars on the window cast a complex shadow that resembled a musical staff and notes. Some of the notes, he noticed, were moving. In the doorway, the bare foot also moved, and Frontenac wondered briefly whether its owner was, in fact, alive.

He turned back to Jean, who had begun again to look at the manuscript. "But instead," he said, "I find myself here to deliver you from this earthly hell. Allowing you to live out your days here could be no favour; but I can hope," he said, lowering his face to within a few inches of Jean's, "that *this* hell pales in significance and horror to the one I'm sending you to."

Frontenac put the heel of his left hand on Jean's head, which he pushed back. With his right hand he drew the knife violently across Jean's exposed throat, opening a long gash which immediately spurted a geyser of dark, dense blood over the manuscript which Jean still held tightly in his lap.

Jean turned when he heard the strains of a distant but familiar music. He knew that piece . . . from what seemed like a long time ago. As the night's shadows began to lengthen in the room, he walked over to the window, threw it open and leaned out, by some magic unimpeded by the bars that had always been there. It was a cool, misty night. There were no stars in the black sky—only two fresh new moons which glowed a dull ochre. Long, straight cerise clouds drifted across their pocked faces. Bursting from the horizon behind them, *gleamed the great domes and spires of a wondrous City. And below the window stood a bizarre figure draped entirely in yellow, his face covered with a Venetian carnival mask of particularly unpleasant aspect. Jean cried out in joy. It was his beloved King finally come, after so many years, to forgive him. The King beckoned to Jean, opening his arms wide in a gesture of love and absolution. Sobbing, Jean pitched forward towards him; as the wind roared past him he closed his eyes and readied himself to join the bosom of his Master.*

Frontenac watched in satisfaction. Jean's eyes widened as his mouth opened to gasp at air that for him no longer existed. His body shook violently as he attempted to breathe but could only make harsh, grinding noises as great red blossoms of blood bubbled at the gaping wound in his throat.

Frontenac stepped back to avoid the surging blood. "I'm sure you won't begrudge me one parting gift, Master," he snarled, as he leaned forward gingerly and ripped the manuscript from Jean's clenched fists. "A souvenir of our last moments together, a remembrance of the blood that I spilled in my sweet Amelie's memory."

He quickly rolled up the gory manuscript and stared as Jean bled and suffocated. "I believe I have an ugly box that will accommodate this perfectly," he said, mostly to himself. After a few moments, Jean stopped quivering and his head lolled slowly over onto his chest, closing the wound in his throat and slowing the flow of blood that was puddling at his feet.

"*A bientôt* Master," Frontenac said, saluting the corpse with the rolled-up manuscript. "If we do meet again, it will surely be in hell." He turned and, hesitating a moment, walked up to the bare foot in the doorway. He pushed it aside with his buckled shoe as he closed the door behind him, choosing not to look at its owner who was, in fact, lying against the wall and singing quietly to herself as she plaited her filthy hair.

Frontenac skipped carefully down the stairs. Relieved to encounter no *hôpital* officials, he crossed the vestibule and quickly exited. Closing the door behind him, he took a deep breath of the comparatively sweet air of an 18th century Paris morning, jumped into the waiting coach and headed for Switzerland.

KING FATHER STONE

Darrell Schweitzer

King Father Stone, under the earth,
swimming in blood to give himself birth.
King Father Stone, under the sky,
gobbled three sons, but won't let them die.
   —Anvastou children's rhyme,
   recorded in the notebooks of Sekenre the Illuminator.

Darkness and thunder.

King Hrosan raged in the night, against the rain and wild wind, against his traitorous sons and their armies arrayed before him. He could not allow the battle to end, not now, not like this. But, in the pouring rain as the darkness closed in, the shield-wall broke and the royal troops scattered, streaming from the field into the adjoining woods, pursued by yelling cavalrymen.

Now the slaughter had truly begun, and the night was filled with the frenzy of it, a second storm of death amid the surging elements.

He cursed his sons' names. He shouted, facing into the wind. No one could hear him.

The realization that all was lost hit him like a fatal blow, numbing him at first, even as wounded soldier is sometimes numbed for a few minutes before the pain comes and his blood pours out.

The king tore off his purple cloak and threw it aside, drew his sword for the last time, and plunged into the oncoming mass of his enemies, striking this way and that, like a swimmer laboring against an impossible tide. In a flash of lightning he saw the mass of struggling men heaving up, washing over him, as ten thousand voices cried out. Trumpets spoke, before the thunder came.

Ahead of him, somewhere, infinitely far away yet almost within reach, swayed the huge, golden standard of one of his sons. He couldn't tell which. Possibly Hrosanian, the eldest, whom the king had once bounced on his knee, whom the king had trained in horsemanship and war, whom the king had discreetly advised in the matter of his first murder.

Or it might have been Hrosantae, or Hroso, or even Delmantine, who was only four years old. It didn't matter. They were all monsters.

He had sired them.

They would tear the Pentarchy of Anvastou to shreds fighting over it.

By the Nine Gods of Righteousness, he cursed them all.

It was time to die.

Something hit him squarely between the shoulders and he sprawled forward. His shield buckled and was torn away. His sword flew from his hand. He rolled over stones, into mud, fumbling for the sword. Someone snatched the crown from his head and he tried to grab it back, but caught hold of a soldier's belt and was dragged some distance through the mud before the man fell down on top of him, dead.

Incredibly, though, King Hrosan did not die. What followed, he tried to convince himself, must have been a dream.

It felt as if he lay in the earth for a hundred years, raging against his sons, while battle sounds filled his ears. Slowly the torrents of blood and the screaming voices in the wind and the footsteps of countless armies wore away the dirt above him, until he looked out on the night sky again, amazed to see the stars.

He lay on a hillside above a battlefield, and wore the fields and forests like bedclothes. His struggled to rise, to break free, brimming with unslaked rage. The earth shook. Stones tumbled and rolled away.

Far below, barely visible in the darkness and rain, two tiny figures were climbing up the grassy slope toward him.

He closed his eyes, commanding himself to awaken from this dream.

Now he lay under a heap of corpses. One by one the corpses were dragged away, and then someone was tugging at his boots.

He raised his head to see what was happening, and tried to laugh, but only managed a coughing snort. A boy was carefully unlacing the purple boots that only a king may wear.

"Don't steal those, child. They're much too large for you."

The boy looked up. The lightning of the fading storm still flickered in the sky, revealing the field strewn with the dead. Squatting down among them, the robber boy—thin, ragged, and barefoot, no more than thirteen or fourteen years old—worked at the king's boot-laces.

About the same age as Hroso, the third of Hrosan's despicable princes, who

would strip his father's corpse even as this boy did.

Dark eyes gazed up at him from a soft, round face. Lighting flickered once more, then darkness came, and the boy held up a cupped hand. Blue flames burned there, sizzling in the rain.

Not a robber then. A ghoul.

Hrosan struggled to get away.

"No, don't," the boy said.

The king wriggled backward through the mud. The boy crawled to follow, holding on to his boot-laces.

"I've come to help you," the boy said. "You don't have to die."

His words were strangely accented, but it was the sense of what he said that made him hard to understand, not his pronunciation.

"What?"

The boy repeated himself.

"This is crazy," said the king. "I am already dead."

The boy shrugged and went on methodically unlacing the king's boots. He pulled off one and tossed it aside, then started working on the other.

"Well, *suppose* you weren't going to die then?" the boy asked. "What would you do?"

Hrosan could not believe he was having this conversation. He couldn't take it seriously. "I'd have my revenge," he said. "No matter how long it took, I'd rip my damned brats from their stolen thrones and grind them up—"

"In your teeth?"

The king laughed. "All right, in my teeth."

"And would you swallow?"

Lunatics speak thus, the king thought. *To them such details are terribly important. Therefore, let one lunatic say to another:* "No,

I would spit them out." He spoke this aloud.

"Ah. So you say. I am not so certain."

Even coming from a lunatic, that made no sense.

The boy threw the other purple boot away. He reached up and pulled the signet ring from Hrosan's finger, tossing that away too. The king was too bewildered to resist.

"If you would achieve your worthy and much yearned-for goal, you must be more than a king, other than a king. Come on. I'll help you. Get up."

Hrosan struggled upright, swaying, his bare feet sinking ankle-deep in mud. He shivered in the wind and rain, coughing. This was all a dream, he told himself again, all some absurdity seeping into his brain as he lay dying. He looked around for his own corpse, but did not see it.

Yet if he were to escape the field alive, from the midst of his enemies, it *would* be a good idea to get rid of every badge of kingship, cloak, crown, ring, purple shoes. That single thread of rationality was more frightening than all the craziness, because it suggested that this might really be happening.

The boy took him by the hand and pulled him along. The boy, too, was shivering.

"What are you, child? What really? Some sort of imp?"

"I am the sorcerer Sekenre and I am not a child."

Hrosan laughed. "If you're a sorcerer, then I'm the master of all the earth. No, you're mad and I am dead."

The boy shrugged. Again, he shivered. "Believe what you want."

They walked on, their feet making sucking sounds in the nearly frigid mud.

"Gods! It's cold!" said Hrosan.

"Flesh must touch, for magic to be true."

This wasn't a dream, Hrosan decided. It was a true vision, such as came to prophets from the gods. It was his task, then, to puzzle out the hidden signs and know the way of destiny.

He walked barefoot in the mud, leaning on Sekenre. Sometimes other stragglers surrounded them in the darkness between the trees. Once, on a forest path, enemy horsemen rode them down, howling through the silver face-pieces of their helmets like metal demon-statues come furiously alive, cutting down stragglers like sodden stalks. But Sekenre opened his hand. A blue flame danced there, and no one molested them, as if they were invisible.

It seemed that for a time that a dead chiliarch walked beside them, his almost severed head rolling horribly, his shattered neckbones grinding while blood streamed over the sunburst-embossed cuirass of his rank. He spoke not from his mouth but out of the gaping wound in his neck, in that universal language of the dead, which somehow Hrosan understood.

Sekenre joined the dead man in conversation, speaking fluently in that same tongue.

The dead man mourned unfinished lives and cataloged the sorrows of this night, remarking how so much suffering, so many deaths, might gather in one place, swirling like a great storm, and assume its own, miraculous life.

He turned away from Sekenre, his head dangling like a sack slung from his shoulders, and to Hrosan said, "My suffering has not ended, Great King. Know that it continues still."

Hrosan replied angrily, "I don't know what you expect me to do about it." He turned to Sekenre for some reassurance, but the boy merely held a flame in his hand and trudged silently.

Then that part of the vision ended, and it was dawn. The rain had receded into drizzle, and the air was thick with slowly rising mist. The boy led Hrosan up a hillside, stepping over corpses, the both of them slipping and sliding in the mud. They caught hold of the stiffening dead to steady themselves, the both of them trembling, exhausted by the cold, their breath ragged and hoarse; both of them utterly caked in mud from head to foot.

Crows gathered on the battlefield, cawing.

Once in a great while, a wounded soldier cried out.

In the dawning light, Hrosan recognized this place. He saw where the enemy's standard had been. He had been walking in circles all night. He regarded Sekenre, who looked like any other urchin, his eyes wide in his muddy face. He yanked the boy to a halt.

"You had better explain yourself."

"I already have. I, a sorcerer, offer you, formerly a king and in your own estimation a corpse, a chance to become something more than a corpse. Do not question. Merely accept."

"You are hardly a sorcerer, child!" King Hrosan swore an angry oath by the Nine Gods of Righteousness.

"You are hardly righteous." Sekenre opened his hand once more. Fire danced on his scarred palms, but without burn-

ing him. "Then again, you are hardly a king anymore, and your sons are hardly model princes. Yet they seemed so, outwardly, did they not?"

"All right. All right. I'll do what you want. If only—"

"No if. No conditions."

Hrosan thought of his sons and their treachery. His rage swelled up. He ground his teeth. "Yes. Do what you will."

Now the vision frayed apart, like a tapestry coming unwoven. Contradictory things happened. He saw Sekenre holding strands of light, twisting them, casting them away. Sekenre got down on his knees and began to dig in the earth with his muddy hands. He bade Hrosan help him, and the two of them dug a shallow grave. Sekenre helped the king into the grave, and covered him cover. Hrosan struggled for breath. He felt the mud in his nose and mouth. He was floating under the ground. It seemed that the limp hands of the slain soldiers reached down and brushed across his face as he passed.

And, dreaming in the earth, Hrosan saw himself and Sekenre kneeling on either side of his grave, in mud up to their elbows. The boy said something he couldn't make out.

And he looked down on two tiny figures, from where he lay at the top of the hill. In the dawn's first light he spied Sekenre and Hrosan, standing over the grave, then making their way onward, up the slope.

He in three places at once, observing and dreaming: walking with Sekenre up the slope, kneeling by the grave, and in the grave.

His numbed feet could not find purchase. He fell many times. The earth shook slightly. Stones rolled past.

"Look," the boy said, pointing.

He looked. Among the massive boulders at the top of the hill, overlooking the battlefield and the forest, a face was revealed, carven there or formed by some impossible freak of nature. He didn't know which. He had no time to consider. He screamed at what he saw.

The face was his own.

It spoke with the voice of thunder. The hillside rippled like a blanket thrown back. Sekenre lost his grip on Hrosan's hand and went tumbling down somewhere out of sight.

The stone face rippled too, and fell down on him, like a tapestry suddenly cut loose.

Hrosan screamed once more, as the great jaws ground him up.

Darkness and thunder.

• • •

He lay in the earth, but he did not die. He lay in the earth, having been swallowed by earth, swallowed by stone, swallowed by himself, but still he could not die.

He lay in the earth, listening to the voices of the land, to the rain caressing it, to the wind, to the rivers flowing. Time passed as a dream and he did not dream; his eyes truly opened as a prophet's are opened, seeing all that the earth had hidden, as he lay in the earth.

He spoke with the dead in the language of the dead.

He raged, and the ground shook. He turned in his slumber. City walls fell. Houses folded in upon themselves.

He raged, because he could hear the voices of men, saying, "The old tyrant is gone. Good riddance." No one mourned the apparent passing of King Hrosan.

No riddance at all, he said, within the earth.

The seasons turned, and in the darkness, in the depths of winter, Sekenre came to him again, walking barefoot on the snow like a ghost, leaving no footprints, blue flame cupped in his hands.

The boy crouched down, and whispered at the grave of King Hrosan, telling him how his sons had fallen to warring, and now Hrosantae and Hroso had allied themselves against Hrosanian their elder brother and now besieged him in a castle far to the north, high in the mountains, where the marches of Anvastou end in utter desolation and the sun never truly rises.

So Hrosan followed Sekenre for long miles, drifting in the earth beneath his feet, in dreams which were not dreams. Sekenre passed through the besiegers' camp as if invisible. The occasional tentpole swayed and toppled as Hrosan slid beneath.

The castle gate opened for them. Sentries cried out in alarm and rushed to close it, but no one saw Sekenre pass through. His bare feet moved silently up stone stairs. Hrosan swam in stone, in the stairs and walls and floors, and the castle trembled very slightly. They passed more sentries in the halls, who did not challenge them. They entered the king's chamber.

It was Hrosanian who called himself king now. He wore his father's crown. He had laughed at his brothers, as Sekenre had told the tale, tapping the crown on the edge of a table to show it was a solid thing, not to be divided lest it no longer be a crown, only scraps of metal.

Now Hrosanian wasn't laughing. He

sat on a wooden bench before a table, by a fire, his most trusted knights with him, a map spread out on the tabletop. He looked miserable and cold, though wrapped in a bearskin.

The new king and his knights were discussing the battle which must come soon, because the garrison had run out of food.

The room suffused with blue light. Hrosanian looked up.

To Hrosan, this was the truly impossible part: He was not dreaming, but in that room, physically, yet not in the flesh. His body was made of stone, living and naked, carven, ripped from out of the earth, massive and invincible as his hatred. He bellowed as he rushed forward, splintering the table, seizing the knights as they tried to defend their lord and breaking them like wooden toys in his stone hands.

He closed his hands upon his eldest son, upon Hrosanian who called himself king, and he devoured him with his stone mouth, grinding him between stone teeth, while his stone ears reverberated with the sound of screaming.

Once he happened to glimpse Sekenre huddled by the fire, wrapped in the bearskin, shivering from the cold. Then, for an instant, Hrosan stood alone in the room, as the fire burned down. Not even Sekenre was there. Outside, sentries banged on the door and shouted.

•   •   •

Once more King Hrosan lay in the darkness, naked and cold, his body incorruptible and unchanging.

His son Hrosanian lay with him.

"Father, I cannot describe how much I hate you."

"And I hate you."

"You taught me by your example, how to grab what could be mine and *make* it mine. You taught me that a king does what he must and will, and makes the laws afterward, fitting them to himself like a cloak."

"You have learned well, and become a king, and therefore I must hate you endlessly, my son."

The father Hrosan rolled over in the darkness and devoured his son Hrosanian once again, until he felt the other's anguish within his mind. The two of them fused into one, became one being, filled with hatred and with rage, like a storm colliding with another and doubling in strength.

But he was not otherwise changed.

The king's mind filled with memories that were not his, with lusts and fears. But he understood them. They were like enough to his own.

Then he lay in the earth for another year, dreaming, listening to the snows melting, to the rivers swelling in their courses, to the sowers in their fields, to the beasts driven to pasture, and to the tread of soldiers as the armies of Hrosantae and Hroso marched down from the mountains after their inexplicable victory.

•   •   •

That summer, Sekenre appeared in the forum of the Eastern Capital, a ragged, muddy-footed boy with tangled hair. The townspeople ignored him, and chattered on of prices and crops, and of politics: how Hrosantae and Hroso had divided the kingdom and would probably be at war soon. Nobody knew what would become of Delmantine, the youngest son, or of his mother, the old king's second wife, Queen Theodatas. Somebody would probably kill them.

Sekenre sat among the beggars on the steps of the temple of the Nine Righteous Gods, a tiny knife in his hand as he carved a piece of wood. He ignored the passing traffic and did not call out, until at last he had finished his work. Then, without a word, he held up his finished carving for a richly-clad lady to see. It was a delicate bird, lifelike in every detail. When he touched the tail, the wings opened. The lady exclaimed in delight.

"That's very pretty," she said. She took it and gave him a silver coin.

He turned the coin over in his hand after she was gone. The image on it was that of King Hrosan, and the inscription on it celebrated his eternal victory.

On the following day, Sekenre carved a wooden fish with a jointed tail and a mouth that opened and closed.

The day after that, a frog. Then a mouse. Then a tiny man who played a flute. Sekenre showed another lady how to hold the wooden man into the wind to hear the music of the flute.

Then a master carver came to him and examined his latest work, a wooden skull the size of a grape with a hinged jaw and every tooth carefully detailed. "Young man," he said. "You are very talented. Come and be my apprentice. You shall work in my shop."

Sekenre smiled and shrugged his shoulders and went on carving.

"Don't you know," the carver said, "that I am carver to the king? I provide him with sacred images for holy festivals. An apprentice of mine can go very far indeed."

"What king might that be?"

The carver was taken aback. Then he said, slowly, "I can tell that you are a for-eigner. Yes, I see it in your face, and I hear it in your voice, certainly. Know, then that our king is the noble and righteous Hrosantae, second son to the former king, Hrosan."

Sekenre did not ask what had happened to the first son. Instead, he put his knife and the wooden skull away and went with the carver. He dined in the carver's house that evening.

But first the carver's wife insisted Sekenre have a bath. She had her maid fill the tub. Sekenre waited for both women to leave the room, but instead they pulled off his clothes and the maid threw them out the window into the rubbish heap behind the house. Then they shoved him into the tub and scrubbed him with a brush so hard that he yelped.

They paused, clearly disturbed when they saw that he had scars all over his body, as if he had suffered terrible wounds, that the palms of his hands were seared, almost featureless, and part of one of his ears was missing. The maid seemed about to say something, but the carver's wife merely shook her head, made a *tsk*-ing sound, and went on scrubbing.

"Where are you from, Sekenre?" the lady asked.

"From very far away."

"And how old are you?"

"You wouldn't believe me if I told you."

"And your father and mother?"

"Both dead . . . My mother, yes, my father, sort of."

"Well, either people are dead or they aren't."

"Sometimes."

She looked at him strangely, then dried him with a towel, while the maid fetched one of the carver's old shirts, which Sekenre could wear as a robe, with the sleeves rolled up. It came down past his knees.

The carver's name was Rogatis, his wife Godfinna. Sekenre became the most brilliant apprentice Rogatis had ever seen. The delicacy of the boy's carving, the detail he could bring out in wood or ivory or even stone, was truly incredible.

"You are already a master," he said. "How did you learn so much?"

"I practiced for a long time."

"But, one so young—?"

"I had a long time."

When the summer festival arrived, Rogatis and Sekenre dressed in their finest clothes, Godfinna endlessly fussing to make sure Sekenre was presentable, and the carver and his apprentice carried the products of their labors on special trays, to be offered to the king.

"What sort of man is this king?" Sekenre asked, as he and Rogatis made their way through the crowd, toward the special pavilion which had been set up in the city's forum. There King Hrosantae sat on a golden throne, the temple of the Righteous Gods at his back.

"They say that our lord is a hard man, one who has been forced to do many grim things, but sometimes he sorrows at the memory of what he has done, and his future actions are moderated. More than that . . . it is not wise to say."

"Ah."

One by one the craftsmen of the town presented their gifts to the king, to be paid, blessed, or driven out by attendants with clubs.

Rogatis knelt before the throne, bowed his head, and offered up his tray. An attendant carried it to the king, who removed the cloth covering and beheld a wooden locust, ten times life size, with jeweled eyes. As he watched, it came alive, stirring. It rubbed its legs together and sang.

"We are pleased," said King Hrosantae, "if a bit puzzled. What does this thing signify?"

"It is hard to explain," said Rogatis, who could not explain it at all, because it was Sekenre's work he was passing off as his own.

"My Lord," said Sekenre, interrupting, then continuing before anyone could hush him for speaking out of turn, "there is no explanation to be had, nor any needed. The thing is merely a marvel, and the delight is in its construction. That delight, then, is conveyed to you."

"You are a bold one," said the king.

A courtier paid Rogatis several gold pieces and ushered him away. Then Sekenre offered up his own tray, speaking again out of turn. "But this, Lord King, has a more obvious and immediate meaning."

The servant carried the tray to the king and the king removed the covering.

He screamed. The stone carving he beheld was the perfect image of his father's face. It opened its eyes, and the eyes were filled with fire, as if a tiny furnace raged within. The thing spoke in a voice he had not heard in a long time outside of his nightmares, saying, "Second of my brats, I come for you."

And it swallowed him, sucking him into its stone mouth as if he were made of smoke, grinding him in its stone jaws.

The wooden tray and the king's crown rattled to the pavement before the throne.

•   •   •

Beneath the earth, old king Hrosan

conversed with his second son.

"I truly hate you."

"And I hate you, Father, but I wish it were not so. I reigned long enough to learn that a king is a kind of slave, bound by his throne and his crown as if they were chains, while all men flatter and secretly abuse him. It wasn't worth murdering you."

"Is that supposed to be comforting? Am I supposed to embrace you in a flood of tears and beg your forgiveness even as I offer you mine?"

"I only wish it were so, Father."

Hrosan rolled over in his sleep, in the darkness, and devoured his son once more, and the two of them become one, fusing together, and a new voice awakened in the king's mind, a voice which rebuked Hrosanian, the eldest, who was already there, and filled the king's mind with fears and doubts, even with tender memories. Hrosantae re- turned again and again to the quiet hours as he lay beside his wife and queen, whom he truly loved, and whispered to her that the evil was all past, that it was no longer necessary for him to be cruel.

"I wish it were so," she had said, and Hrosantae, the second son, and Hrosan, the father, both wept at the memory of that, while Hrosanian, the eldest, scorned them both.

In his unending dream, old Hrosan saw Sekenre before him, swimming in the muddy earth. "Have you had enough?" the boy said. "Is your revenge complete?"

Hrosan did not answer for a long time. He too was like a swimmer, fighting against a tide of memories and sorrows and hesitations that were not his own. He clung to the memory of who he had been, old king Hrosan, father to four sons who

had betrayed him and overthrown him in a battle, one night in the rain.

Remembering this, he at last was able to say, "No, my revenge is *not* complete," while that part of him which was Hrosanian laughed mirthlessly and that part which was Hrosantae wept.

"My work isn't complete either," said Sekenre.

•   •   •

"We all know what must be done."

The conspirators met in a vault below the palace in the Western Capital. Gorhinglas, a great lord, spoke for them all.

"We cannot have civil war again. Already, the barbarians press us hard. Nor can we afford a regency, which will only mean weakness and further division. Therefore the child Delmantine and his mother, the former queen Theodatas, *must die.* Our Lord Hroso must sit on the throne *alone,* or we are all done for."

The others nodded in agreement.

"My boy is the key to it," one of them said. "My stepson, Sekenre, an orphan whom I found it useful to adopt. He has become young Delmantine's playmate. He can get us into the right chambers. He can steal keys and open doors. If necessary, he can do the job himself."

All this while the boy Sekenre sat on a stone bench nearby, idly playing with a cup-and-ball. He paused. "Oh yes, Stepfather. I will finish everything for you if you want me to."

Therefore, that same evening, Sekenre went to the carefully-guarded wing of the palace where the queen's chambers were. This was all that remained of her kingdom, the only place where she could feel safe, surrounded by her few loyal followers. King Hroso would never dare storm the place, for fear of the outcry. It was officially given out that he shared the diminished Diarchy of Anvastou equally with his half-brother, Delmantine, and honored the boy's mother, Theodatas, as if she were his own.

In fact the two were Hroso's prisoners, though he had not figured out how to dispose of them.

His loyal courtiers proposed to solve the problem for him.

So Sekenre went, dressed in an embroidered blue robe, white leggings, and silver slippers, with all the appearance of a prince, for Delmantine had given him some of his own clothes. The supposed stepson of a minor lord, he was deemed harmless enough. He said he was fourteen. The young king Delmantine was now twelve, fatherless under circumstances best not discussed, for eight years.

Sekenre was the boy's only playmate. The two of them studied together. They shared games and secrets. Sekenre told the most amazing stories, to Delmantine alone, and performed even more amazing tricks, but only if Delmantine swore never to tell his mother.

Further secrets, which Delmantine offered to Sekenre in exchange, included knowledge of numerous sliding panels and hidden passageways, and the possession of a set of keys.

Now Sekenre slipped into one of those passageways, opened a panel, descended a marble, spiral staircase fashioned like a writhing serpent, unlocked a door, and admitted Lord Gorhinglas and the twelve other conspirators, including Ouen, his own stepfather, into the crypts below the queen's suite. All of the noblemen carried drawn swords.

"We'll gut him like a sheep," somebody said.

"Don't relish it so. It's a horrible thing we must do," said Lord Ouen.

"But necessary," said Gorhinglas. Turning to Sekenre, he said, "Lead us on, boy. Do not lose your courage and do not think to betray us. There will be a great reward for you when this is done."

Sekenre knew that most likely the reward included being gutted like a sheep, but still he led them among the tombs of kings, past effigies of conquerors who had made Anvastou great. He turned another key. A creaking door swung wide of its own accord, and all of them but Sekenre had to duck their heads as they crowded into a low-ceilinged chamber where unfinished tombs lay open and empty. It was a musty, damp place, with no sign of recent construction, though the carvings were only half finished, and marble chips and abandoned tools lay all about.

"Why have you brought us to *this* accursed place?" Gorhinglas demanded.

Indeed it was accursed, for these tombs had been prepared for the most recent rulers. Here, stretched as if asleep, lay the image of the oldest son, Hrosanian, but the tomb was empty, because Hrosanian's body had never been recovered. And no one had figured out what become of Hrosantae either, for all there had been witnesses, many of whom went mad with fright at the memory of what they had seen. So the second brother's tomb was hardly begun, the image on it no more than a scratched lump, and a sigil was cut into it, to ward off evil.

The conspirators made gestures with their hands, for luck.

Nearby were smooth, unadorned tombs where one day, quite soon it was earnestly hoped, Queen Theodatas and her son Delmantine would rest, without ceremony, hastily buried and forgotten.

"Again I asked you *why* you have brought us here?" said Lord Gorhinglas. He looked angrily at Ouen first, then raised his sword to threaten Sekenre.

"My Lord," the boy said, "Delmantine and I come here often, to play our games."

"I always knew the brat was unwholesome," one of the assassins said.

"Here especially is our *favorite* place." Sekenre brought them to the tomb of King Hrosan, where a huge stone effigy of the king's face seemed frozen in the middle of a great shout. "This is part of the game." He put his head into the gaping stone mouth, and his voice suddenly came from several directions at once. "You do it. Try it yourself."

Sekenre drew his head out again and turned to Lord Gorhinglas. Several of the assassins eyed the stone face uneasily.

Gorhinglas paced back and forth testily, ducking his head. "I don't have time for stupid games. Now you say that Delmantine will meet you here this night?"

"Yes, Lord, very soon. All you and your friends have to do is hide yourselves and wait. But first, come and look inside here. You must, to understand a very great secret."

Gorhinglas sighed and put his head into the stone mouth.

The stone eyes opened, burning with blue fire.

The other lords screamed as the stone jaws ground to life, as the mouth closed and the headless body of Lord Gorhinglas flopped to the floor, spouting blood like wine from a ruptured skin. It was too late for any of them to escape.

The stone face spoke with thunder, stunning them all, pronouncing their individual dooms. The castle shook. Stone and plaster rained down from the vaulted ceiling. The walls came alive, the other crypts bursting open as stone hands reached out to seize each of the twelve.

Then King Hrosan sat up, bursting through the lid of his own tomb, grown hideous huge like a centipede with twelve arms.

He devoured what he had caught.

•   •   •

When Sekenre entered Delmantine's room, the young king rushed to embrace him.

"What's happening? What's going on? Mother is so afraid."

"It's just the earth trembling."

"No, it's more!"

Then Queen Theodatas came in. She embraced both Delmantine and Sekenre. "Righteous Gods protect us! I sent one of my maids to King Hroso, but she couldn't get in. The soldiers were all running around. She heard the king *screaming,* she said. Oh! It is the end of the world!"

"He is not screaming anymore," said Sekenre.

Queen Theodatas let go of Sekenre. She looked at him strangely and drew her son away.

"No, I suppose he is not. But how do you know, Sekenre?"

Outside in the corridor, the footsteps of something far heavier than a man thundered nearer and nearer. Guards shouted. Metal clanged on stone. Men screamed.

"*Sekenre!*" the queen shouted. "*What do you know?*"

He held out his hands to show that

they were empty, but they were not empty, and blue flames danced on his palms. "I only know that this is the end of what began eight years ago."

The queen screamed as the door splintered and the astonishing, marble monstrosity which wore her late husband's face clawed its way in. Its lips, chin, and many fingertips were smeared with blood.

Even Sekenre turned away from the sight.

Once more, in a voice like wind and thunder, King Hrosan pronounced inexorable doom. He stepped forward, the floorboards straining beneath his weight.

Sekenre turned back to look, and several things happened at once. Delmantine drew a dagger and stood in front of his mother to protect her. But Queen Theodatas shoved him aside and hurled herself into the monster's arms, shouting, "No, husband! No! He is too young. He is innocent! Take me instead!"

In the frenzy of his rage King Hrosan took her, his stone jaws grinding until his whole face was covered with her blood.

Delmantine shouted something and struck with his dagger. The blade broke. He cried out again, and held up his arm in a useless attempt to shield himself, but then paused and lowered his arm, because the monster did not attack him. Instead, it paced back and forth, turning from side to side, its hands waving chaotically, tears flowing from its stone eyes. It bowed down, hunched beneath the ceiling of the chamber, and the stone face spoke his name, and said something more, in a voice which was his father's and wasn't, in many voices at once. He couldn't make it out.

He thought he heard the word "for-give" before the floorboards snapped and the stone thing crashed into the vaults below.

The young king reeled back from the edge of the broken floor. Sekenre caught hold of him. The two of them struggled, rolling at the edge of the opening. Delmantine held the broken stump of his dagger to Sekenre's throat.

"Don't do that," Sekenre said. "If you kill me, you will become as I am."

•   •   •

Sekenre swam through the earth and whispered in King Hrosan's ear, where he lay turning in the sleep which partook of both death and dream.

Hrosan wept, grinding his teeth. A babble of voices came from his mouth.

"I am a father who devoured his sons. I am a mother who died for her own. I am Gorhinglas. I am Ouen. I am Hrosanian, Hrosantae, and Hroso. I loathe the evil within myself, the thing that I was and have become. Merciful Sekenre, help me. Let this thing end, now. Please."

"It's not so simple, mighty king, is it? You are all those things, all those persons. King Hrosan remembers them, and they remember what Hrosan remembers. All of you are mixed together, like differently colored paints stirred into a pot. The color of Theodatas is the color of genuine love, and that, King Hrosan, is beyond your imagining. Your son Hrosanian was just like you. Hrosantae resembled you much, but he had a conscience. Hroso whimpered like a beaten animal, fouling himself in terror. That, too, O king."

"End my pain. What can I do?"

"Delmantine still lives. Is your revenge complete? Do you want me to arrange something?"

King Hrosan screamed in his own voice now. Far above, rivers leapt their banks and the stone faces of cliffs broke and tumbled. The skies were filled with fiery portents.

"I just want to die. I want this to be completed at last."

"No, I cannot allow that. It would ruin the project I have undertaken."

Then King Hrosan raged, and called out to the merciful gods. They did not answer.

"As for me," said Sekenre, "I am merely a sorcerer, and not necessarily merciful."

•   •   •

So Sekenre led King Hrosan, in the dream which was more than a dream, walking to and fro in the earth and up and down in it. Hrosan felt the rain falling on him, for the earth was his flesh. He felt the earthquake roiling in his guts. And he felt the entire world, at his feet, spinning among the stars before the gods.

He walked barefoot on an old battlefield, where white bones poked up out of the mud, where ghosts wandered aimlessly like mist. He gathered those ghosts to himself, the chiliarch and all the rest, devouring them one by one, filling himself with the sorrows and longings and memories of ten thousand lives, growing great with pain and remembered joy, with wisdom and foolishness, until among the many voices within him, only one was King Hrosan, whom the others dimly recalled.

And they spoke to him, Hrosanian, Hrosantae, Hroso, and Theodatas, and the slain ten thousand, and they told him what he must do.

"We are alike, you and I," Sekenre said, a little later. "To become a sorcerer, you have to murder other sorcerers. Then they fill your head, and you and the others become one, and their secrets are your own. I began as a boy, tricked into murdering my own father, as part of one of *his* schemes, so that he might hide from his enemies in my body. Therefore I became him, and I knew all those others he had murdered, and all those *they* had murdered. We are legion, of countless names. The outward body does not change, but only after a long struggle could I sift out that memory which was the boy Sekenre, and cause the others to whisper the name of Sekenre within me, until their whispering becomes a great harmony, and I became again, at least in part, that boy who was Sekenre, who was both brave and afraid, and who killed his father and was swallowed by him."

"I am not sure who King Hrosan is anymore."

"Let him be known as the Fortunate One, for he has one advantage a mere sorcerer does not."

"What is that?"

"He can disgorge what he has swallowed."

In a dreaming time which is forever and no time at all, King Hrosan walked barefoot on the surface of the River of the Dead, with ten thousand restless ghosts in his mind and in his belly. Sekenre walked with him a little way, but then turned back, and Hrosan continued on his own.

The dark water rippled out from his feet. The crocodile-headed *evatim,* the messengers of the Death God, hissed at his passage, but did not molest him.

He passed from the country of dream into the country of true death, which lies in the belly of the Devouring God, Surat-Hemad, whose mouth is the night sky, whose teeth are the stars. There, in the land of the dead, kneeling in the holy mud by the bank of the river, Hrosan disgorged his sons, his wife, the chiliarch, and the ten thousand, laying them to rest, to be unmade.

But when he returned from out of the god's mouth, he retained those voices and memories inside his mind, like echoes, for all he had laid them to rest.

Sekenre waited for him on the river's bank.

He spoke to the boy in the language of the dead. "Do you understand, truly, why you have done these things?"

"We are so alike. I thought that in you I would find the answer to myself."

Hrosan shook his head sadly. "We are not alike at all."

Sekenre wept. "I feared it would be so."

"But you do not regret what you have done."

Very softly, the boy replied, "No."

"Thank you, Sekenre."

The boy made a gesture with his hand, to acknowledge the presence of holiness. Then he took the king by the hand and led him up out of the earth.

In the dreaming time, this took almost forever. In waking time, a single night had passed, and just before dawn Sekenre saw the king walking in the sky, behind the stars, in the company of the gods. The Righteous Nine were there, and many more, gods and goddesses, some with the heads of animals, one with a face formed all of flowers, some who were winged.

Sekenre covered his eyes, because it was not meet that a sorcerer, who is unclean, should look upon the gods.

That morning he sat alone on an old battlefield amid broken stones, writing the tale of King Hrosan into a book. The air was cold.

•   •   •

Who comprehends the work of sorcerers? Surely not they. Most especially, not they.

—Attributed to Tannivar the Parricide, from the notebooks of Sekenre the Illuminator.

THE FARE

Chris Vail

Dawn had come up, though not like thunder. No, it was too sneaky for that. A sneak attack, because it was immediately hot as hell. One of those days when you first notice it's day because you feel the heat, not because you see the light. Like most of the arguments Gus found himself in.

Arguments? In his line of work? A cabby couldn't afford to be argumentative, not with fares. No, Gus saved it for the other guys at the dispatching point. And then he had to save it for the mirror, because his mouth finally got him kicked out of the cab company. So now he flew solo.

Competing with his old colleagues, he'd had to carve out his own niche. Partly he got by on a growing group of regular clients, those who just couldn't face driving into the City and wouldn't be caught dead on public transport. People who were well enough off to use his services on a regular schedule, not rich enough to afford an actual chauffeur. Besides this, Gus swallowed hard and roamed the streets during the graveyard hours when most drivers had given up and hit the sack. There was sufficient slack to take up that way, he'd found.

But the resultant schedule was crazy. It played hell with romance, social life, everything else. He hadn't seen most of his friends for months. Hell, he hadn't had regular bowel movements in months. It was getting to him. Maybe he

ought to try to become a chauffeur, a kept man with some leisure. But then there'd be the suits. Gus couldn't stand the suits those guys wear. Butlers on wheels. No, probably not for him.

He didn't even know why he tried it, but he slid the air conditioner stud to the right, hoping it might do more than agitate the stale air in the taxi. Somehow when it did that it seemed to just make the damn thing hotter. Nothing happened. Nothing much was happening on the road either. He'd just dropped off a passenger at Newark International. He'd had to wake up the fare when he got him to his terminal. Turned out the guy's flight wasn't due to take off till comfortable mid-morning. He was one of the type who have to get there a few hours early "just in case."

It might have been someone else's first fare of the day, but it was going to be Gus's last. He'd been at it all night, all stagnant humid, stifling night. Now it was time to head home to his waiting empty apartment in the south end of Montclair. There he looked forward to a good day's sleep. He'd learned to sleep through just about anything the day could throw at him. Fatigue, he'd discovered, was by far the best sound-proofing.

He'd finally emerged out of the labyrinth of highway ramps, construction tiger-teeth, and dyslexic clumps of competing road signs and was on his way to the relative calm of the pre-commuter

Parkway when he saw the guy. At first he couldn't decide whether the lone, tired-looking figure was flagging him down or just thumbing. Gus's rig wasn't obviously a cab till you got a look at the livery plates. As he neared the man, he figured it didn't matter much either way: if the poor slob just needed a ride, what the hell. Gus was going his direction. His good deed for the day. Maybe his fairy godmother would reward him. Yeah, reward him by laying off the plague of bad luck.

He pulled off onto the shoulder, slightly overshooting the man. As the guy sped up and trotted to the waiting vehicle, Gus tried to get a reading on him from what he could see in the rear-view. Once he sat down, he wouldn't be able to give him more than a cursory glance. Gus fancied himself not a bad cold reader. When people rushed into a taxicab, it was like you were catching them in the act somehow, whatever the act might be. They still radiated a particular momentum. He liked to try to peg them. Once in a while a stray bit of small talk would confirm his theory. Sometimes not. Most often he never found out one way or the other. Just the same, he was pretty sure he usually got it right.

This guy would take some figuring. What the hell was he doing wearing a suit jacket and a tie, his collar still buttoned up to the neck, in this inferno? He must have been walking this way for some time. And yet there was no sign of the profuse sweat you'd have expected.

The passenger was now reaching for the door handle in a way that struck Gus as slightly unnatural, yes, with what seemed to be the wrong hand. He had set a briefcase on the pave while he opened the door, and now he had recovered it and was hopping in. Into the front passenger seat. Gus didn't like that usually, unless he felt he wanted to be able to keep more of an eye on his fare.

Holy Christ! Gus felt almost physically forced back against his door by the impact of a blinding, choking stench that had entered the cab along with the man like an invisible companion. He felt as if he were helpless under water, suffocating. Hell, he didn't care, couldn't afford to care, what the man thought, he rolled down the window as fast as he could and stuck his head out, gasping. In fact his reeking passenger seemed not even to notice. Maybe the reaction was too common for him to think much of it anymore.

The damnedest thing, after the initial shock, was that the guy didn't even smell like B.O., not even like vomit, aromas Gus had had to adjust to in his line of work. No, it seemed more like toxic fumes from a burning chemical factory. Or he guessed that's what they must smell like. But how could a man smell that way? What was the deal with this guy?

He was on the road again but hadn't noticed. Automatic pilot, force of habit. The stench now seemed to have subsided somewhat. He no longer felt the subliminal sense of panic as if he were in danger from it. Maybe the inrushing air from his window helped. He'd definitely have to get that air conditioning fixed. He noticed that his eyes were tearing up and reached up to wipe them. Gus, normally no stickler for etiquette, felt strangely self-conscious about his obvious display of discomfort and disgust. Ironically, he felt *he* was being offensive by his behavior. Time for idle chatting, to create the pretense of normalcy. Besides, it might provide a clue to what was surely a genuine mystery.

"It's pretty early to be hitching." Gus still wasn't sure if this was a paying fare. Maybe this way he'd find out. "And you're not even beating the heat—it's roasting out there. Sorry the AC isn't working too well."

"Coming from the City." The profile did not change. He stayed looking directly ahead like Roosevelt on the dime. That much Gus's peripheral vision told him. He waited for more, but the man seemed to have said his piece. So Gus decided to prod him again.

"Guess you had an all nighter, huh?" That ought to make the man say something, if only to define what an "all nighter" might or might not mean in his case.

"Don't want to talk about it." Gus nodded. Then why'd you mention it? Now Gus was thinking the guy had been having some sort of illicit rendezvous when his car broke down or was stolen. Yeah, that would explain why he hadn't phoned anybody he knew to pick him up. Didn't explain everything though.

"Jeez, I didn't even ask where you're bound! Where can I drop you?" With this, the driver noticed he had come in sight of a toll plaza and reached over to his change-filled ash-tray. Another surprise. Looking down, he got a look at the man's left hand: no fingers or thumb. Gus had been the kind of kid who'd embarrass his parents by pointing out the handicapped and disfigured like they were specimens in a zoo. He'd never made fun of them or anything. Just the opposite: they frightened the hell out of

him. Even when he was old enough to know better. They still seemed to him repulsive medieval freaks, God help him. God help them. In fact you'd think the Almighty owed them some help. Gus was ashamed of his reactions, his cringes, but he couldn't help it.

If the man answered his forgotten question Gus didn't hear it. He had started to feel that he was not in his familiar cab, that instead, as in a dream, it had all become some kind of roller-coaster or creepy fun house ride.

The fare repeated himself, impassive face still pointed to twelve o'clock high. "I said Jersey City. Headed home. Tell you the streets once we get there."

The man got out in a neighborhood Gus didn't care to linger in too long. Sort of belied the guy's suit. But then it was common that you saw the poor dressing their best to affirm some vestige of old world dignity. Just as common to see jobless weirdos dressed meticulously, a bit too meticulously. Gus didn't hesitate to put this guy into that category.

As it happened, he didn't even discover whether his passenger had been a hitch hiker or a paying customer. Didn't stick around long enough. It was sufficient pay to be the hell rid of him. He was out of there the second after he heard the passenger door slam shut. On the way home Gus could think of little else than his luck that the strange rider had not offered any concrete danger. With certain people you just couldn't know what to expect. They might attack you at the wheel, never mind that they were endangering themselves just as much. But it didn't happen.

And that smell! Now he figured he knew the difference between "stink" and "stench." Back on the Parkway he felt the clouds dissipate. The cab interior was suddenly free of the smell. And he felt free of his fear. It was only then that he realized how he must have suppressed both during the time he had the fare with him.

Back home, he dropped into the unmade bed still fully clothed, having only kicked free of his shoes and fished out wallet and keys so he wouldn't roll over onto them as he slept. Outside his window, elderly black folks were beginning to drift down the steaming sidewalks toward a charity food drop down the block. Grandmas had pesky kids in tow, but none of this bothered Gus as he hailed a fast cab for slumberland.

The phone woke him six hours later. He usually liked to get in an even eight, but this time he didn't mind. the ring only interrupted a series of dreams, already more than half forgotten, of people with no fingers, people losing fingers in all sorts of ways, accidentally biting them off, or something crazy like that. To hell with that stuff.

It was old Widow Langsdorf. She was calling on short notice for a lift into the City to her favorite beautician. Here she lived in one of the wealthiest towns in the Metropolitan area, but apparently nobody in Montclair, even in snooty Upper Montclair, was good enough for her. That or brand loyalty, Gus thought confusedly as he gave her the brightest okay he could manage. Sure, no problem.

He did his best to make himself presentable; respectable was too much to ask of him this early (though for others it was mid-afternoon). And besides, the old lady couldn't see clearly enough to tell the difference. In fact, she probably had to take the hair dresser's word for it. He cranked up the cab again, stopped by the Exxon and headed for the other side of town, where they even had a different zip code.

Gus dropped off his charge at the curb, where a door man met her and accompanied her inside. A door man! At a hair salon! He'd taken people to hotels with less classy service.

Looked like he was in luck. He usually had to park a couple blocks away in a high-priced hourly lot, but today, even at this hour, there was a spot, a legal one, not far away. He pulled in, extinguished the ignition, and slumped down for a nap. He'd have to wait for the old bag, but she paid for the time.

The rough shoulder tap of the door man brought him awake. He jumped out of his seat and helped Mrs. Langsdorf into hers. As he shook his head awake, he heard her tell him that today the routine would be different. She wanted to be taken to LaGuardia, where she would meet relatives who had gathered to welcome another family member off a plane. Then she would go with them to Long Island for some big party. So he could leave by himself from the airport. Sure.

Dropping her off, he haunted the pick-up area. Didn't take long till his turn. He managed to pick up an arriving passenger at the curb, played the obligatory moment of dodgeball with the other arriving and departing vehicles, and took her a short distance into Manhattan. Gus caught himself at one point starting to drift from sporadic small talk to telling the story of the strange fare from early in the morning. But then he realized it just wasn't fodder for idle chit chat with a customer. He clammed up for the duration.

He was set to cruise the streets for

more business, but somehow he felt he just couldn't face any more. The heat was still too oppressive. God's thermostat must be on the blink. This was just too damn much. To hell with it, he was going back home early. At least his one room air conditioner was working, though none too steadily in this weather.

He sat in the traffic approaching the George Washington Bridge for forty minutes, way too long, though he was feeling too enervated to get pissed off about it. Still, he probably should have listened to shadow traffic.

Finally he was past the expanse of the Hudson, spilling out of the bridge with the other cars like ants from a hill. He aimed for 46 West which would take him to the Parkway South.

You couldn't say it was a familiar face; he'd never gotten a good look at the guy's face. But he saw a familiar form. There was the briefcase, the same clumsy arm-waving to flag him down. And he even seemed to be buttoned up to the chin again. What were the chances of this? And could the guy possibly have recognized his cab? Why would he want the same one even if he did?

It was just because the whole thing made no sense at all that Gus decided to take a chance and pull over. It was deja vue as the man trotted for the door. Gus braced himself for the smell. It wasn't nearly as strong this time, but still strong enough to make you suspect more than one driver had taken a whiff and left the guy stranded. But it had reduced from a stench to a stink, and Gus was intrigued. He braced himself and realized he was feeling just like he used to as a kid in the splatter flick theatre: afraid, terribly grossed out, yet peeking through the fingers he'd held up to shield his eyes! Fingers.

"Hey, long time no see, huh?" Silence. Again: "Like, fancy meeting here, huh?" Gus spared the passenger a sidelong glance. This time the man, his face a poker, did at least turn to him long enough to mumble, "We met?"

"Sure! Don't you remember just this morning? Over near Newark International. You travel fast, I'll say that! Jersey City, right?"

"Jersey City?" the man asked in his monotone. Sounded like he'd never heard of Jersey City before.

"That's where you're going, isn't it? Like this morning?"

"No. Headed home. I live in West Orange. Give you the street address when we get there."

To this there was nothing to say, nothing Gus could think of. He just drove on in silence, onto the Parkway, turning off for 280 and reaching West Orange before long. Pretty much the same route he'd have been taking home anyway. And it was a hell of a lot closer to his own destination, Montclair, that Jersey City was.

He was confirmed in his judgment that the guy was crazy. Either he really didn't remember Gus's picking him up scant hours before, or he felt he had to deny it. Either way, it was what you'd call crazy. Poor schmuck.

Tensing as if for a blow, Gus glanced down involuntarily to the deformed left hand. Only this time there was no hand, only a wrist stump that did not even protrude beyond the white cuff. Holy Jeez. What had happened to the poor bastard in the last few hours? Well, Gus sure as hell wasn't going to ask him. He didn't think he'd want to hear the answer.

They drove into a shaded suburban street lined with two and three storied houses. Not mansions, but not post-war suburban split-levels either. How could this guy even know anyone here? But he'd said this was his own address. Maybe it was. Maybe he had some errand in Jersey City, but this was home. No, no, damn it, Gus remembered well enough that he'd said he lived in Jersey City.

Wordlessly the man reached one-handedly into a pocket in that queer way that makes you realize how many little gestures involve two hands. The movement seemed as routine to the man as it did strange to Gus, like when a cripple offers you the wrong hand for a shake. Takes a moment to get used to.

He hadn't told the man what he owed and didn't pause to count the change now. He left in less of a panic than before, but no less puzzled. Even more. He thought he caught a rear-view glimpse of the guy giving him a look as he drove away. Somebody had come down the front walk to greet him, but then Gus had to turn the corner.

In the ten minutes it took to get home, Gus half-heartedly tried to place a couple of jigsaw pieces together, but the edges wouldn't come near fitting. Could the guy be suffering from some sort of rot that caused the terrible smell and made it necessary to amputate first his fingers, and then the whole hand? Not likely. That wasn't outpatient stuff. He couldn't be commuting into New York for that.

He felt like having a beer. None at home. And it wouldn't be bad having somebody to talk to. Why not hit Tierney's?

The juke box was on louder than Gus

liked, but at least that meant the place was populated, and with normal people. He took his drink, which he now realized was scheduled to be the first of a series that night, and drifted over to a half-empty table. It wasn't long before Sam sat down beside him. Sam had been night dispatcher at Gus's old cab company. He had a drinking problem, periodically swore off, but continually tempted fate by hanging out at places like this. He just couldn't extract himself from the only social world he knew. He seemed sober these days, his slight slur by now an acquired accent. He was still smoking, another habit he wasn't quite ready to try to kick. One thing at a time, he had told Gus more than once.

It was good to see Sam, good to see Gus, they agreed. Conversation drifted from nowhere in particular to nowhere else in particular. Sam was about to get started on his bitch of a girlfriend and how he had finally wised up and broken off with her—again. And Gus decided to head him off with the story, such as it was, of his odd passenger. He felt almost ashamed, as if Sam were a priest in the confessional and Gus had some sin to own up to. He guessed he felt somehow wrong for his perverse curiosity about matters best left undisturbed. And then there was his deeply rooted horror of the deformed and the grotesque. He knew it was childish, and he felt a sense of child-like shame at catching himself feeling that way.

The story didn't take long. Sam stared. "Yeah? So what happened?"

"Jeez, nothing exactly *happened*. But don't you see, the guy was so strange. The smell. And his pretending not to know me the second time."

"Come on, man. Do you think you're that memorable? Do people even look at a cabby long enough to remember him?"

"Yeah, I guess that's true. But even after I told him it was me, he denied it. And what about the addresses? Did he move from Jersey City to West Orange in less than a day?"

"Look, who cares! Maybe the guy's some eccentric who has two addresses. Or maybe he's lying about one of them and can't keep his story straight. You said he's crazy. Maybe he has a different house for each personality!"

Sam seemed to think this was pretty amusing. His rattling laughter quickly turned into a sputtering cough. About that time, Marian, his ex-ex-girlfriend came up from behind to comfort him with a pat on the back and a kiss. If Sam had bothered telling her he was giving her the kiss-off, she'd been too drunk to hear him. Gus could see which way things were about to go, so he picked up his empty mug and returned to the bar for his first refill.

In the next weeks Gus grew more and more preoccupied. That was easy to do when all his off-time, just about, was spent alone. He found himself saying less and less to his fares, even his regulars, who asked him what was wrong. He wasn't lying when he said nothing was. At least there was nothing specific. But to himself he had to admit that he couldn't leave the puzzle of his mysterious passenger alone. He couldn't resist toying with it, like you do with a scab or a throbbing tooth. Maybe it was absorbing him more than he let on. It was time for a vacation, he supposed, but he worked for himself. There was no one to give him one, with pay that is.

It was one afternoon crawling through traffic on the Verrazano Narrows Bridge that a possible answer popped into his head. Maybe the guy's parents lived in Jersey City, but he had his own place in West Orange. Sure, then both would be "home." Gus was tempted to dismiss the whole thing. Even if he couldn't be sure he had figured out the truth, his theory would seem to give him an excuse to file the thing away and forget it.

Only he just couldn't. He realized that it was less the mystery of the thing than the lingering thrill of fear and disgust he felt, like a kid who can't get to sleep after watching Chiller Theatre. Every time you'd drift off, you'd remember your fear of having a nightmare and wake back up.

The summer blast furnace gradually exhausted itself, and right on schedule, about the third week in September, the furnace shut down, just like the ones in Pittsburgh. From then on it was a lot cooler. The days were shorter, and Gus benefitted from the invigorating snap in the air. He was feeling pretty good for the first time in a long time. Whatever it was that had been bothering him seemed to have left for a vacation of its own.

But then he came back from vacation. There he was, early on an October morning, at almost the same spot on the highway Gus had first seen him. He might have been walking from Newark International or from the City, Gus couldn't tell. He felt a sense not so much of deja vue as of fatalism as he resigned himself to slow down for the peculiar figure. This time the man had no jacket over his primly buttoned shirt. He must have been pretty cold, especially if he'd been out walking any length of time.

The Good Samaritan instinct took over. In fact, the big reason Gus's job, monotonous to some, did not drive him nuts was a secret feeling he'd always had that he was doing good giving people the rides they needed. A chance to take a load off their feet, to get where they were going instead of showing up late or having to walk. He was doing them a favor, and when they rewarded him by paying the meter's suggested donation, all the better. But he'd really have to admit that his curiosity had got the upper hand this time. He just had to know what was going on, to see the next development if there was one. And at the same time, Gus was somehow sure that whatever secret there might be, he would regret learning it.

Here he was riding shotgun again. He didn't smell nearly so bad this time, but did certainly smell odd, as if he'd bathed in a strong disinfectant—or insect poison, maybe. Another smell you just didn't associate with human beings. Gus decided to say nothing he didn't have to say, to see if the man would betray by any word or glance that he knew him, that he remembered his driver. No hint came. Then he thought of the hand, and he knew that there was something he was subconsciously trying not to notice. Shamelessly, he glanced down. The arm ended at the elbow, where the white sleeve was pinned back.

Now the passenger was looking at him, his nondescript face registering no sign of emotion or irritation. This is what Gus secretly feared, to be caught red-handed being a tactless gawker. He couldn't think of anything at all to say. What he heard himself saying was "I'm sorry." Sorry for the man's amputation? For his own cruel gaping? He didn't know. No response.

But the fare did say something: "Headed home. Nutley. Let's get there first, then I'll give you directions." Gus wasn't surprised. It seemed inevitable. He got off Route 3, drove up East Passaic, onto High Street, not the most direct route, but he was kind of confused. Then down to Center Street, turning left at the T-section, past Ralph's Pizza and under the train trestle, left through the gates and curbside before a bigger house than the one in West Orange.

Did the guy pay him? He couldn't even remember. Didn't care. But he felt certain he had not discharged this passenger for the last time. He was home in no time, Nutley being even closer to Montclair. Hell, he wasn't even getting as much per ride from the guy! He chuckled at this, but it sounded too much like nervous laughter.

What was going on? In the weeks that followed, he began to spin improbable tales. Began running them by the prostitutes he visited. They didn't even pretend to be interested or to know what he was talking about. But that didn't stop him. Could the guy be going into the City, to some seedy section, where a cult of some sort met? He was secretive, after all. And what went on there? Maybe this guy was the chosen sacrifice to Satan or something. Only they were taking him apart piece by piece. Maybe they all had a bite, him included. And the smells? Could be anything; who knew what those cultists did behind closed doors? It was all pretty far-fetched. But what mundane explanation would fit?

One day just before Thanksgiving Gus decided to drop by the garage of his old cab company. Some ignored him, others looked suspicious. He heard a couple of mutters ending with "that jerk." But he didn't care. He cornered a few of the guys, whose names he couldn't quite remember, as they were sitting having coffee and smoking.

"Listen, you guys, I just want some information, you know, just to compare notes. Any of you picked up a real strange guy in the last couple months? Strange like he reeks to high heaven. And he's always wearing the same white shirt buttoned to the chin. Always has a briefcase with him. He's out along the highway, as if he's hitching when you pick him up.

Blank faces so far. Not uninterested, but ill at ease. Why did he want to know? What was wrong? Their expressions said that much.

"You'd remember him; he's had the fingers on one hand cut off, then the whole hand, then the forearm."

One finally confessed that he had had a strange fare a month or so back, a guy who stank so much that the driver had just pulled off onto the shoulder and ordered him to get out. This wasn't something the driver felt comfortable admitting. If reported, he could be in big trouble. You can't just abandon passengers you don't happen to like. He had gambled that the man himself wouldn't report him, and he hadn't. Now he was willing to risk other drivers knowing it. It must have bothered him, and his own curiosity was showing now.

Another, hearing this, confided that he didn't recall any such odor, but decades of smoking had pretty much dulled his sense of smell anyway. But only the other day he had given a lift to a one-armed man, who might have been dressed that way, though a shirt and tie were by no means uncommon. Did he remember where he had dropped this man? Nutley? No, just over the Montclair town line in Bloomfield, a two-family house not in the best of shape.

"Hey Gus. Did this guy rob you or something? Then what's the big deal? If you see him again, just don't stop for him, right? Am I right?" Gus lamely agreed, not bothering to explain why he couldn't just let it go like that. And the thought occurred to him that he *had* been avoiding the guy, all his life. That wouldn't work any more. He couldn't explain it to them because he couldn't have explained it to himself in the first place.

Gus awoke one early December morning with a strange feeling, as if he had an appointment he had forgotten. He was pretty good with his schedules, as he had to be. Even kept a duplicate schedule book in case he lost the one he usually carried. He rubbed the sleep from his eyes, his nagging hunch getting harder to ignore. So he checked first one of the schedules, then the other. No, nothing there. And yet he felt he ought to get up and get behind the wheel. He headed out with no particular destination in mind, just waiting for something to pop into his head. Meanwhile he would try to stay alert for business. A couple of cross-town drop-offs, nothing much. One was a bag lady who didn't even offer to pay. But he had expected she wouldn't. Good Samaritan, after all.

Without consciously deciding to, he turned down Watchung Avenue and went up to the entrance to the Parkway North. Maybe he'd have a long lunch at Paramus Park. He kind of liked the greasy lamb they served in one of the Food Court stands, even though he knew he'd have bad indigestion. But the exit came and went. He idly continued on till the Parkway turned into the Throughway. It was a bright day, and not a bad one to see some of the sights of the Hudson Valley. Maybe he'd stop in Nyack, where they had all those strange antique shops. But what would be the point of that? He couldn't afford any of that stuff. He continued across the Tappan Zee Bridge, paid the rip-off toll at the end of it, and tried to decide if he wanted 287, maybe go on into Connecticut the way things were headed. Yeah, why not?

There he was on the cross-hatched triangle at the turn-off for 287. He stood unsteadily on a crutch. His left arm was missing from the shoulder. With his right he held onto the crutch which stop-gapped for his missing right leg. He certainly needed a ride. What was he doing there? Why didn't anybody stop and help the guy to safety?

Then Gus noticed a state trooper's car, but it was headed away from the scene, as if to urgent business elsewhere. It was up to him. This must be his appointment.

He earned a few surprised honks from swerving cars, as he didn't really have room enough to get the cab completely out of the way. He threw the car into park and carefully got out, walked around the vehicle toward the man. Though his now-familiar face was as blank as before, he seemed to be waiting for Gus, like a kid waits for Mom to pick her up after school in the parking lot.

"Hey!" he shouted to be heard above the rushing cars. "Looks like you could use a lift. Here, let me get the door." No briefcase this time, nor any jacket. But

every button was on duty. All Gus could smell this time was the stale odor of Vitalis on the carefully kempt and combed black hair.

Once he closed the driver side door, it shut out most of the noise. Gus fastened his seat belt and watched for an opening in the traffic. It might take a while, and he was antsy. He wanted to have this, whatever it was, over as soon as possible. Let's get this show on the road, huh?

Okay, there we go, into the maelstrom. "Where can I take you, mister?" Did the passenger know him? Did he feel any need to explain, whether by a lie or by the truth, the obvious question mark his body had become? No way to tell.

"Home. I'm headed home. Upper Montclair. Don't want to talk about it."

"Sure, no reason you should. Tell me the street address once we're in town, okay?"

"No, I'm all right." The man said as Gus offered to help him into the house off Valley Road. The house was spacious this time, and the man hobbled with manifest difficulty into a side door, probably to an apartment. Many of these old mansions had been honeycombed with partitions in recent years. As Gus drove away, it registered that the windows of the place had been boarded up. Were they doing construction? He recalled no sign of scaffolding. Was the guy squatting in a temporarily tenantless house? But why then would he advertise the fact by pulling up in a cab at the front door?

Did the guy really change addresses so often? And what the hell was happening to him? Creeping gangrene? Cancer? He'd never be allowed out of the hospital if it were spreading at that rate. It was all impossibly strange. And yet Gus was used to it. It was a tough nut to crack, but Gus viewed it as more like a puzzle. He had to. It was impossible to deny the strange things that had happened in recent months. So he had to take them as given, like it or not, understand it or not. It was like a detective novel. There would simply have to be a solution sooner or later. He just wanted to figure it out before he reached the last page. It might be some kind of advantage to be prepared. He drove the rest of the way down Valley road to the South end of town where he lived.

It was mid-February. Gus had given up driving. His landlord thought he was sick and was apparently willing to cut him some slack, at least for the time being. He was a good guy, and Gus had never stiffed him before. He didn't want to now. He just felt he could not get out of bed and face—whatever it was life required of him. He listened to the radio quite a bit, the same Oldies station he used to listen to in the cab. The songs were so familiar to him that he practically did not hear them anymore. Mere memories.

He didn't bother to turn the radio off as he turned over to go back to sleep. He might have dozed off, for how long, he didn't know. But it was night. He enjoyed sleeping at night again. He was even going to the crapper regularly again.

So there were some advantages.

What woke him was a soft scratching against the inside of the closet door. Gus's apartment was pretty small, so nothing was too far away to escape his notice. At first he figured it was the damned mice again. De-Con just didn't cut it anymore. Little mutant bastards probably ate the stuff for dessert by now.

But, no, it was too insistent, too regular, too *intentional* for that. As he got up out of bed and steadied himself, he felt more annoyed than anything else. Some cat in the heating ducts? No, he had radiators. He couldn't think what he had done with the flashlight, but once his eyes adjusted, he realized the room was easy to navigate simply by the leaking light of the greenish street lamps outside.

By the time he had taken the few steps needed to go down the short hall and grasp the closet doorknob, it had come to him. He formed no specific mental picture, but he wasn't surprised to open the door wide and trace the dim outlines of what he saw there. It was a limbless torso, propped against the back wall, as against a cushion of fallen shirts and slacks and a parka. Only the head remained jutting out of the truncated stump. The voice was familiar, though he had never heard it say more than twenty words. "I'm home," it announced.

FAMINE WOOD

Stanley C. Sargent

After receiving several polite brush-offs and having a few doors slammed in their faces, two novice members of a religious group that recruited door-to-door were shocked to find themselves warmly welcomed by Abe Camden, an elderly gentleman who responded when they knocked upon the door of his somewhat isolated farmhouse. Not only did the man appear receptive to their pitch, he ushered them into the parlor, seated them both in an antique 'love seat' and invited them to present their well-rehearsed rhetoric. The farmer, thought the visitors, must be desperately lonely as everyone else they had approached had abruptly turned them away.

The pair bombarded Camden with religious information, then tried to draw him into a discussion of the finer points of their church's teachings. But to their surprise, the initially quiet and patient old gent suddenly seized the conversational reigns. Before they realized what was happening, Camden had taken off at a verbal gallop that defied interruption.

"I've heard of Yahweh's Children before, but you are the first I've ever met," he began. "And I appreciate you young fellers coming all the way out to the middle of nowhere, especially considering Madland County's reputation. Sometimes I think the great state of Ohio would be greatly relieved if this here county just up and disappeared!

"Now don't let on like you don't know what I'm talking about, 'cos *everybody's* heard rumors about how, shall I say peculiar, the folks of Madland are, and I admit there's a certain amount of truth to what they say!

"No sir, there ain't many willing to venture into these parts, particularly not to spout religion to the locals! You see, folks 'round here don't cotton much to what you'd call traditional religion. We've got a church here, but I suspect you'd take exception to the liberties Reverend Petersen takes with the Lord's word in his sermons.

"None of my family were church-goers, so I've got to admit I never give much thought to religious matters. But after listening to you two, I'll allow there's a certain appeal in some of what you say. I'm particularly interested in the part o' your spiel where God forgives even the worst of sinners when He's asked to."

The wizened old character paused for a moment, seemingly lost in thought, then chimed in again loudly at the first indication that either of his guests was about to make comment. "You see," he continued, "something happened a number of years back that still weighs heavily on my mind. I just can't seem to shake the memory of it, though I was not much more than a foolish teenager at the time. I know I'd feel a whole lot better if I just put it all behind me, but to date I haven't been able to do that.

"If you boys wouldn't mind listening, this might be a good opportunity to get some of it off my chest. They say confession's good for the soul, and at my age a man's got to fess up to his shortcomings least they haunt him all the way to the grave . . . and maybe even beyond."

The two youthful guests glanced at each other nervously. The worm had obviously turned in an unanticipated direction. They had been instructed to maintain total control of the situation while peddling their propaganda, but they had never actually gotten this far before and thus had no idea how they might regain the upper hand. All they could really do was sit quietly and listen, least the old man think them rude. If they passively listened and observed, maybe they could discern some means to deal with such dilemmas in the future.

When his visitors did not protest, Camden smiled. "No doubt you never heard of Famine Wood, but that's no surprise as folks don't like to talk about the skeletons in their closets, and the people around here are no exception. Well, I don't mind telling you about Famine Wood, but first I'm obliged to provide you with a bit of background.

"The first whites in the Ohio territory were nothing but trappers and fur traders, daring souls who risked their lives avoiding the various native tribes in hope of stockpiling enough cash to make good lives for themselves when they returned to more civilized parts back East. Still, there was one brave group of six families that lit out on the Ohio River to look for greener pastures. They made it all the way down here to the Mad River Valley before dropping stakes. Now this was right when the French and English

were both finagling to claim Ohio for themselves. They were ruthless, turning the Indian tribes against each other 'til it turned into a full-scale war, the French and Indian War. The Shawnee, Miamis, Wyandots, Delawares, Mingos and others were already fighting each other tooth-and-nail, not realizing they were being used by the Europeans to bolster their own claims to the territory. So when the six families arrived, they were all on their own in the midst of a wilderness war zone.

"The Miami tribe let them settle here but only in a part of the forest they considered unnatural. The Miamis claimed their 'Master of Life' had warned them to avoid that particular patch of wood 'cos the spirit of the place was only half-formed and not willing to accept intruders. The Shawnee held the territory before the Miamis, and they too claimed their 'Great Spirit' had warned them away from the place for the very same reasons. So the Indians didn't mind the white families as long as they restricted themselves to the wood they themselves considered off-limits. The settlers were neither French nor English, but the Indians figured the spirit would surely make short work of them. And, as it turned out, that proved to be the case."

Camden paused to settle in his seat, confident his listeners were becoming caught up in his tale. He continued, "Everything went pretty well for the newcomers 'til 1762, about a year before the end of the war. Crops failed throughout the entire Ohio Valley due to a terrible drought, and it wasn't long after that famine set in. To top it all off, both the Indians and the Europeans began to drop like flies from the smallpox. The Miamis turned to the English since they'd helped them send the French packing, but the Brits ignored them. The Miamis in turn didn't give a hoot when the settlers looked to them for aid. Before winter was over, every member of the six families had either starved to death or succumbed to the killing force of the cold.

"The British settlers that came along later found the wretched remains of the six families and buried their bodies right where they lay. They vamoosed out of there right after, claiming something about some of the bodies didn't look quite natural. Even later, when more whites moved into Valley, they heard enough spooky stories to stay clear of the Wood where the families were buried. A cloud of superstition hung over the place. Some said the soil was tainted, having soaked up the excruciating hunger of those who starved to death, and that's how the place came to be called Famine Wood.

"It wasn't until more than a score of decades later, during the Civil War, that anyone actually entered Famine Wood again. Word got around that a rogue troop of Confederate soldiers had been spotted in the area, and they probably saw the Wood as a good place to hide out while they'd planned some mischief. They were seen marching into the Wood, but nary a one of them ever came out. It was like they just vanished into thin air!"

The speaker halted to clear his throat before plunging back into his narrative. "My buddies and I weren't old enough to have good sense, and we were curious about the yarns we'd heard concerning the Wood. We didn't believe in ghosts, so despite the warnings, we were stupid enough to decide we'd go out there and take a look around just for the heck of it.

"Me, Roscoe Masters and Tom Tucker had grown up together, so we were more like brothers than friends. Heck, it was Roscoe that first showed me a man's pecker was good for more than just draining his bladder! But it was Tuck and me that ended up fooling around two, three times, 'til I got tired of such shenanigans. Tuck didn't want to give it up, but, well, I got this sudden interest in girls. Roscoe swore Tuck never got over me and, mind you, though I wouldn't have hurt the lad for worlds, I just considered it puppy love. Well, no doubt you know how it is with us fellers at that age!"

Noting the scandalized expressions on the faces of those he addressed, he further remarked, "Then again, judging from the set of your mugs, maybe you don't know. Don't know at all!" The old man laughed uproariously.

While Jim struggled to regain composure that he might offer some intelligent response, Mike maintained his dumbstruck silence. Jim finally tendered awkwardly, "Ah, so you, ah, committed the sin of homosexuality and that's what's been haunting you all these years?"

Camden hooted, "Hell, no! There ain't no sin in chums getting intimate! Tuck and I shared everything; I mean *everything*, and I don't regret it for an instant. The bond we forged was a rare and precious one that neither one of us ever regretted!" Agitated now, he closed his eyes and shook his head. "I guess I shouldn't of brought it up," he harrumphed, "I just felt it necessary to emphasize the fact that Tuck and me were as close as two folks could be."

Seeing the way the two inched away from each other in the love seat, the frowning Camden continued his narration. "Anyways, Roscoe picked me and Tuck up at my folks' place around noon that day, and we took a round-about dirt road to the Wood so none would suspect we were going there. Not that anybody would have tried to stop us if they'd seen us; they'd have just figured we were out of our minds and left it at that.

"Roscoe parked the truck 'neath a nest of trees right up next to the seven-foot storm fence that closes 'round the eight or nine acres of Famine Wood. Just who put that consarned fence there is anybody's guess; it's been there since long before anyone can recall different. All around the Wood is open pasture, so we guessed the fence was meant to keep livestock from straying into the Wood. But we were soon to learn the hard way that there was a damn sight more to it than that!"

The speaker lowered his voice and paused to observe his guests momentarily. As expected, both remained silent, obviously intrigued by the unraveling tale.

"That darn fence was a bitch to get over. Storm fences are made of real fine metal mesh that's meant to catch debris so as to clog up when there's a flood; that way it acts like a dam to keep back the water. It's pretty flimsy, though, and wobbles like crazy when a body tries to climb over it. The outside was clean but for rust, as you'd expect, but the inside was bound tight with vines and brambles enough to hide pretty near every inch of the actual fence. Seemed like more was trying to get out than trying to get into the place.

"Once inside, everything changed. The Wood's a shadowy, sinister kind of place where nature's turned all dark and brooding. Put me in the mind of some kind of ancient, evil womb.

"Right off we saw the trees were bigger than any we'd ever seen, and a dang sight older too. The bases of some of those giants were as big around as houses and the trunks were twisted and deformed something awful. For sure none had suffered the hand of man since the time of those doomed first settlers. The boughs of those trees met way up above, locking together like spooky fingers serving to blot out as much sunlight as possible. What feeble light managed to filter through lent a nasty, kind of jaundiced glow to that awful place. The air was stagnant, still and muggy, making every move a sweating effort. We got the feeling right off that the place was watching us, ready to pounce at the first opportunity. I admit I had to fight to keep from turning tail and heading for the openness still visible on the other side of the fence.

"Aside from the buzzing of insects, it was unnaturally quiet in there too, like a graveyard at night. Not a single bird sang in the whole place, and we never saw any kind of animal either, which was awful strange. There should have been squirrels, rabbits and chipmunks everywhere in a wood as wild as that, but we didn't see hide nor hair of a single creature the whole time we were there, not even a 'coon nor a possum. We couldn't help but feel we were trespassing where we ought not to be, but we still kept going.

"Darn near every inch of the boggy ground was covered with a layer of dead, rotting leaves to a depth of better than a foot in most places, and more leaves were constantly raining down from above, like sallow snowflakes gliding silently through the air. There wasn't much in the way of grass or weeds able to penetrate the leaf blanket, though fungus, moss and toadstools grew all over everything else. And since it was warmer inside the Wood than outside, there were bugs everywhere, flies and gnats. Even the mosquitoes were bold enough to be out and biting in the daylight. What with the yellow light, mugginess and eerie quiet, there was a hatefulness about the place that didn't sit well with us at all.

"But we'd come to explore, and, sure enough, it wasn't long before we came across the remnants of some of those first settlers' cabins. Not that there was much left after all that time but a couple boulder chimneys and piles of decaying logs. One site had three walls still standing, and with a bit of kicking around, Tuck exposed a section of crude flagstone flooring that remained intact. The highest of the walls only came to about shoulder level and, of course, nothing was left of the roof.

"Roscoe struck out on his own, but it wasn't long before Tuck and I heard him let out a yelp. We went running to see what the problem was, only to find him stuck half in the ground, nearly up to his waist, screaming and cursing like all get out.

"Seems those that buried the dead settlers just sort of packaged them up in cheap pine boxes and plugged them in the ground right where they fell, and none were buried too deeply. Roscoe had stepped on one of the makeshift coffins and his foot went right through the rotten wood. His leg was cut up but he'd only started screaming when he tore the lid off the box as he tried to pull free. When his weight was applied to the old bones inside, the top half of the skeleton rose up as if to grab him, the round yellow skull lolling to and fro on the tip of the spine. The sight of the damned thing scared Roscoe nearly half to death, it did! It took some finagling, but we eventually pried him loose, calmed him down and stopped the bleeding. It was obvious to Tuck and me that the main bone in the lower half of Roscoe's leg was badly broken, so we couldn't expect him to walk.

"Well, the two of us heaved and hauled him over to that three-sided cabin I mentioned, but he griped so much about the pain and how the hardness of the stone floor made it worse that we finally lugged him outside the shelter and propped him up against the trunk of an ancient oak. We used a bottle of cheap gin that Tuck always toted around with him to disinfect the wound, but neither of us knew how to set the bone.

"Tuck had the best sense of direction in the bunch, so he lit out for the truck, thinking he'd drive on in and pick us up rather than the two of us carrying Roscoe. If he couldn't find a hole in the fence, he'd find a means to lay it down somewhere and just drive the truck right over it. All Roscoe and I had to do was stay put.

"I parked my butt on the dead log near Roscoe, thinking I'd make a comfy spot for myself by stripping the bark off the trunk. But when I pulled off a hunk, I saw there was a whole slew of bugs lurking beneath, frenzy-feasting on the wood. More ants, grubs, beetles, and mites scrambled off that log than you could shake a stick at; the mass of them had chewed and riddled the wood so much it reminded me more of pulp mush than the remains of a tree. It was enough to make a body's skin crawl, so I chose to plop down a few feet away, on the hard flagstone of the old cabin."

The man lowered and shook his aged head as he emitted exasperated sounds. "Shouldn't a taken him long to get back, but it was over an hour before I heard Tuck shuffling through the leaves.

"I started to ask why he hadn't brought the truck, but the puzzled look on his face silenced me. He grumbled about how walking straight in any direction should bring a body to the fence sooner or later, but it didn't in the Wood. No matter which direction he went, he ended up confused and all turned around until he finally ended up right back here where he'd started. He said he'd felt light-headed and dizzy, but he was still sure he'd been going straight in one direction. I recall him saying it was almost as if the space within the fence was distorted in a way meant to keep anyone from leaving once they were inside, like it was some kind of trap.

"Sounded like nonsense to me, but the sun was going down, leaving us no choice other than to drop stakes for the night right there. We assured Roscoe we'd get him to a doctor first thing in the morning, but he'd gone all quiet, like he was in shock. Tuck and I built a decent fire, then doled out the sorry sandwiches and snacks we'd brought before settling in for the night. Tuck and I decided we'd rather sleep on the cabin floor than stretch out on the open ground, regardless of the hardness of the stone. We'd given up trying to move Roscoe inside with us by then, but we figured he'd be okay since he was only a few feet away from where we settled.

"Judging from the glimpse of moon-light I caught through the thickness of the branches above our heads, I'd guess it was about midnight when something woke me up. The highest limbs of the trees surrounding us commenced to creaking and crackling something awful. But there wasn't a hint of a breeze, which meant wind wasn't the cause. Still, the ruckus continued incessantly for what seemed like at least an hour. All that rustling and moaning in the branches was awful queer, even to a county feller like me; I'd never heard such carrying on before. Tuck sat bold upright and took notice after a bit, but neither one of us dared speak a word. After a while, I got the feeling the trees were sharing secrets among themselves, things we humans could never understand."

The man fidgeted in his chair, a gesture that added odd emphasis to his words. His audience remained silent, anxious to hear what happened next.

"After a bit," Camden mumbled, "Roscoe started groaning in his sleep, almost like he was reacting to the clamor in the trees above. He talked a bit, but I couldn't make out much. I'm pretty sure he cried either "Get out" or "Get away" a couple times, and Tuck whispered that it sounded to him like Roscoe was gibbering something about getting out before it was too late. I'm not ashamed to admit we were both so spooked by all this that all we could do was scoot closer together and try to stop shivering.

"Then it all stopped at once. The sound of the trees and Roscoe's moans cut off at exactly the same instant. If that wasn't eerie enough, all the chirping, buzzing and croaking of the night halted right then as well. It was as if every ounce of life had suddenly dissipated from the world around us. I could hear only Tuck's rapid breathing over the pounding of my racing heart. The two of us lay there, clutching at each other like terrified kids. I guess we nodded off after a while, but we sure didn't sleep soundly.

"Come dawn, I was still nodding when Tuck let out a yell to end all yells. Seems he woke up before me and decided to check on Roscoe's leg before disturbing me. By the time I rushed to his side, he was swatting like the devil at a cloud of big fat blowflies that rose up from Roscoe's leg in a black swarm. They were all over Tuck, buzzing around his head like hundreds of angry bees. We'd cut Roscoe's jeans the night before, slitting the leg from the bottom to just above the knee, so when Tuck'd flipped the loose flap of pant leg aside to check on the wound, the flies that were feeding on the wound came at him. By the time I got to him, I'm not sure whether he was screaming more because of the flies or because of what they'd left behind."

The elderly gent looked much older as he swallowed hard and continued. "You'll recall me telling you earlier about what lay beneath the bark when I stripped it off the oak tree. Well, once the flies disbursed, I could see that Roscoe's leg looked pretty much the gawdawful same; the flesh had turned all soft, yellow and putty-like, and every inch was crawling with maggots, ants and grubs gobbling up the pus that was leaking from the wound. They'd drilled a honeycomb of tunnels into the skin and the muscles so's it looked more like Swiss cheese than a man's leg. I tried to brush some of the bugs off, but I stopped when a chunk of Roscoe's calf muscle tore right off in my hand like meat falling off the bone of a well-done roast."

Camden's eyes closed as he spoke and his body convulsed as the painful memory sent a shiver the length of his body.

The two representatives of religion experienced a wave of nausea as they pictured the scene in their minds. The rather large lunch they had eaten earlier suddenly did not sit so well in their stomachs.

"Roscoe'd been lying on his side. I guess I must have been whimpering like a baby when I rolled him over and called to him by name. I thought at first he might be in a coma, but one glimpse at that blank, bluish face told me he was a goner. He wasn't breathing, his tongue lolled out one side of his mouth all gray and black, and when I lifted an eyelid, the pupil had rolled back in his head. It was a shock more horrible than I can describe.

"You can't imagine how Tuck and I felt," the farmer exerted, "Roscoe, our best friend, gets his leg all messed up, yes, but not bad enough to kill him, and certainly not to change him into a corpse that looked for all the world like it had been laying there dead for days! None of it made sense to us, no sense at all! Tuck, well, he got sick as a dog, but I just stood still for a while, not really feeling anything but numb. When I finally snapped out of it, I tried to make sense of what was going on as we couldn't just stay there like that; we had to get the hell out of there as fast as possible."

He sighed heavily. "I finally was able to speak, though for the life of me I can't recall what it was that came out of my mouth. Next thing I knew, Tuck was pulling at me and screaming that we had to escape that accursed place before we ended up like Roscoe. He rambled through a plan he'd been mulling over, a way we might be able to reach the fence. He'd once read something about space being curved or something like that, and that's what he thought was going on around us in some distorted way. That's why, he said, he'd ended up back in the same place when he walked in a straight line earlier. If we walked toward the rising sun, he said, and used it as a guide, we should be able to stay on course and make it to the fence. I didn't know anything about curved space, so I didn't understand what he was talking about, but as I had no better idea, I went along with his idea.

"We didn't waste any time covering Roscoe's body with a coat before high-tailing it out of there. The body reeked of compost and there wasn't no point in trying to take him with us. We daren't run, since the leaf-covered ground was damp and mushy soft in places. We were scared we might trip or fall and end up not being able to walk, so we took it slow and easy."

"You must have been frightened out of your wits!" cried the sympathetic Mike, noting how very frail their host suddenly appeared.

In confirmation, Camden yelped, "More than words can relate! And if it wasn't bad enough already, Tuck accidentally kicked up the remains of one of them fool Johnny Rebs who'd hid in the Wood during the Civil War, the bones still wrapped in a tattered uniform. We feared we were going to end up the same way."

Sighing, Camden rested further back in his seat.

"Tuck must of been right about the curve thing 'cos before long we spotted the fence. We couldn't help but start grinning, whooping and hugging like idiots, we were so relieved."

His voice dropped to a hush as he confessed, "It was then I knew Roscoe'd been right about the feelings Tuck and I shared for each other." Shaking his head sadly, he added, "It's a crying shame how folks tend to refuse to admit their true feelings for one another until it's too late." He shot a challenging glance at his audience. "There ain't no finer bond than what we had, and it didn't make a lick of difference that we both were fellers. You youngings'll be damn lucky if you ever have a relationship that even approaches what Tuck and I had, regardless of whether it's with a woman or another feller."

Mike detected tears glittering at the corners of the old man's eyes. He turned to his frowning companion and was relieved to see he wasn't going to comment.

"Please, go on, sir," Mike urged, "we're listening."

The wary speaker nodded, acknowledging his gratitude.

In calmer tones, Camden complied with the request. "We lit out for the fence at top speed, but when we were less than three or four yards of reaching it, the ground beneath our feet began to heave and drop down and away. It sucked at our feet like quicksand, trying to drag us down into the rotten leaves and soil. We could barely pull our shoes free long enough to keep moving. Before long, we were sinking all the way to our knees in the muck.

"I heard once it's best to stretch out flat over quicksand, so I called out to Tuck as I sprawled out onto the surface as best I could, telling him he should do the same. He was too panicked to pay attention to what I was saying though, and before long he'd sunk darn near up to his waist."

Camden's listeners trembled with anticipation.

"I sprawled out over the soft dirt in an attempt to reach a gnarled-up tree root jutting out of the ground. I managed to anchor myself by holding on to it. I don't know how I managed it, but I slowly pulled myself across the muck, crawling up the root to the trunk of the tree. Once there, it took every bit of strength I had, but I climbed up to the first big limb. Then I shimmied out as close to the tip as I could so's my weight would bend it down toward Tuck. I threw my weight into the branch to make it bob up and down, all the while calling out for Tuck to catch hold of the end of it. If he could get a tight grip on the tip, all I'd have to do would be back up and let the branch pull him up out of the spongy ground. Once we were both on the limb, we could shimmy up a bit higher to a branch that stretched clean over the fence. We could scramble to safety without having to set foot on the tainted earth again."

As he struggled to continue, the older man's voice betrayed an even greater solemnity. "Tuck'd been swallowed up beyond his waist, nearly to his armpits, but he still managed to get a grip on the nodding limb. I held my breath and commenced to retreat back toward the trunk."

The old man suddenly stopped, as if he were incapable of going on with the story. To the relief of his listeners, however, he continued after a moment. "He started rising up, just like I'd hoped,

but he didn't respond when I called out to encourage him to hang on. Something about his silence gave me the willies and I feared he was about to lose hold. I thought about inching out to catch his hand, but every time I moved forward at all, Tuck's weight drew the branch back down toward the muck. I couldn't see much in the dim light and the damn foliage kept slapping me in the face, but his body started to twirl around in a circle at one point. He managed to get his belt off using one hand and whipped it around the branch, securing his wrists so he could slide a little at a time without fear of losing his grip. That belt was probably the only thing that kept him from tumbling back into the grasping earth below. He slid a couple times, but I could see he was gradually rising up and pulling free, which gave me cause to take heart. I'll never forget the terrified, pleading look on his face when the shadows parted just long enough for me to make out his features. I called out softly, encouraging him by telling him he was doing fine and we'd soon both be safely out of that hellhole."

Camden suddenly choked with passion to the extent that he was forced to stop until he could regain his composure.

Finding himself confronted by a much older stranger completely overcome with emotion, Mike leaned forward compassionately to whisper, "It's okay, sir. Take a deep breath and then just take your time; there's no need to rush. It must be very painful for you to relive such a horrendous experience." He then glanced at his companion, noting the irritated impatience apparent not only in his cross-armed position but in his expression as well.

Camden again nodded to silently acknowledge his gratitude for Mike's sympathetic words. After a weighty silence, he managed to resume his narrative in agonized tones, "Tuck's head popped through the greenery so I could finally see his face clearly; I almost didn't recognize him. He began crawling toward me, but then he turned to peer behind momentarily before crying out as if in agony.

"When he looked back at me, his face was even more contorted, like he was in unspeakable pain. He uttered something I couldn't make out. I asked if there was something more I could do to help him as I reached out with one hand, ready to grab him at the first opportunity. All he did was groan and scream at me to leave him behind and not look back."

Wiping the tears from his eyes as inconspicuously as possible, Camden sat upright in his chair, declaring loudly, "To this day I can't recall exactly what happened next. All I know is that I must have scrambled up to the higher limb and run like a jackrabbit. Hank Danner stumbled across me toward sundown on his way home from hunting pheasant. He said I was sitting on the ground crying and jabbering like an idiot just a few yards from the fence. When he tried to get me to my feet, I started screaming and shrieking like a madman to the point he finally had to knock me out. Right before he'd spotted me, he'd passed Roscoe's truck, which was parked right where we'd left it. He dragged me to it, tossed me in the back and drove straight to the Sheriff's office. When I came to, the doc gave me a shot to calm me down enough to allow me to describe what had happened as best

I could, but there wasn't anything they could do until the next day since nobody's fool enough to set foot in Famine Wood after dark.

"The following afternoon, the Sheriff and a couple others came back with Roscoe's and Tuck's bodies. I was kept locked up for nearly a year after, but not for any crime; the Sheriff declared that, after what they'd found in the Wood, there was no way I could be held accountable for either death. Still, they kept me under wraps until they felt confident I wasn't going to do myself any harm.

"I've never been able to remember what possessed me to turn tail and abandon poor Tuck there to die, though I've tried 'til it hurts. No matter what the Sheriff says, 'til I actually can recall what happened, I can't forgive myself. I can't believe I'm such a coward that I could just up and leave my best friend to die," he choked, "but maybe I am."

Contrary to everything the church taught about how to present himself as a missionary, Jim could contain himself no longer. He jumped up abruptly and shouted, "Mike, we're leaving, right now! I don't believe a word of the swill this old bastard's been spitting out." Turning to address Camden, he yelled, "You're mad as a hatter, you know! You'd have to be crazy to believe the story you just told, and the worst part is, I think you actually do believe it's true! But it's not, it's garbage, all of it. There's no such thing as a man-eating wood, and if you're convinced what you're saying is true, then you know what that makes you, don't you? Not just a coward but a murderer as well. I don't care either way, I just know I'm getting out of here right now. Come on, Mike, let's go."

Mike made a feeble attempt to calm his friend, despite the reeling confusion Camden's confession had set off in his own brain, but Jim was determined.

Camden simply sat and stared at his accuser, unable and/or unwilling to even try and defend himself.

Jim pulled Mike to his feet and all but dragged him to the door. He turned as they exited to shout one further remark. "If there's even a shred of truth to that black fantasy of yours, Camden, then you better hope God can find it in his heart to forgive you because I sure as hell couldn't."

Pulling his friend roughly along, Jim marched to the car. He jumped inside, slammed the door and started the motor immediately. Fearing he'd be left behind, Mike hopped into the passenger seat.

• • •

Jim prattled on incessantly about how Camden had suckered them into wasting an entire afternoon listening to a load of absolute drivel. The old codger, he declared again and again, was obviously insane and probably should be put away.

Mike, on the other hand, felt troubled and downtrodden over the entire experience. He was certain they had abandoned an extremely lonely man in desperate need of counseling and comfort of some kind. What was the purpose of their missionary work if it wasn't to help troubled people like Camden find some sort of inner peace. Mike found his companion's attitude contemptible, and he was ashamed that he had allowed Jim to rail so caustically at a man unable to defend himself. The disillusionment he felt toward his partner had reached its zenith by the time they reached town.

Immediately after Jim dropped him off, Mike phoned Reverend Pauly, explaining the events of the afternoon and Jim's tantrum-like reaction. When the Reverend sided with Jim, Mike immediately proffered his resignation, not only from the missionary work but from membership in the church as well, explaining that he now realized his personal goals radically conflicted with those of Yahweh's Children.

• • •

Three days passed before Mike found an opportunity to return to Madland County. The pain he had seen in Camden's face haunted him continuously during those days, and he was determined to apologize and do whatever he could to undo at least some of the damage he and Jim had inflicted upon the old man. Mike had taken a few psychology classes in college and was convinced Camden was an extremely disturbed man, despite the fact that Mike could not bring himself to accept Camden's tale of horror at face value. Obviously something dramatic had happened to the man that had left him grievously traumatized and in dire need of help. Mike hoped that, given further opportunity to speak with Camden, he might be able to discover the underlying cause of the man's guilt and, with any luck, help him find a way to deal with it. It is impossible to predict how any particular person will react in an emergency, and surely the authorities would have pressed charges had they deemed Camden guilty of any wrongdoing.

It was only when he pulled up to Camden's farmhouse that Mike's determination began to fail him. The front door and windows had been boarded-over and the walkway leading to the front porch was cordoned off with yellow police tape. After staring dumbly for a few moments, Mike spun the car around in the dirt driveway and returned to the main road. Unable to just let the matter drop, he headed directly for the small police station he recalled having passed a mile or so down the road. He prayed he and Jim were not responsible for any sort of tragedy.

• • •

Mike parked in front of the small, rundown building labeled Madland County Sheriff's Office, got out of the car and nervously approached the door. His knock elicited an immediate response from somewhere inside as a voice called out, "It's open!" He entered, suddenly unsure of what he would say to the capable-looking officer seated behind a cluttered desk.

Without looking up, the officer asked, "What can I do for you?"

Mike's hesitation caused the man to glance at his visitor. A look of moderate surprise crossed his face when he did not recognize the face of the young fellow standing before him. "You lost or having car trouble, son?" he queried.

"No, sir," Mike mumbled, noting the officer's uniform identified him as the County Sheriff, "nothing like that." He paused momentarily before blurting out, "I've just come from Abe Camden's place and, seeing the house closed up and cordoned off, I just thought I should check to make sure Mr. Camden is, well, all right."

"I can't say I've seen you around here before. Mind if I ask who you are and why you're so interested in Abe Camden?" inquired the Sheriff.

Camden had obviously been right about outsiders not being overly welcome in Madland County. It occurred to Mike that maybe it had been a mistake to come back after all, but now it was too late to turn back.

In gentler tones, the Sheriff advised, "Take it easy, son. I'm only asking because Abe's been holed up in that house all alone for so long that I'm surprised to learn he had a friend."

The sincerity apparent in the man's voice had the desired effect; Mike identified himself and explained how he had come to know Camden. He explained that he had come back to check on the old man, to make sure he was okay. His friend, Jim, Mike further related, had reacted poorly to an unbelievable tale Camden had told them, and Mike confessed he felt bad about the way Jim had treated him.

When the Sheriff asked if Camden had told them about his experience in Famine Wood, Mike nodded enthusiastically. He started to repeat what Camden had told them, omitting only the part about his abnormally close relationship with Tuck, but he did not get far before the Sheriff waved for him to stop.

"I know the rest, son. I know it only too well. Before I say any more, I think I should straighten you out on one important point. You referred to Abe as an old man, and that's quite understandable in light of the way he aged prematurely, almost overnight, after the incident he described to you. Truth is, I'm thirty-two and Abe was five years my junior. You seem to have the impression that Abe and his friends went to Famine Wood twenty or thirty years ago when, in fact, it was only seven years ago. I was one of the two deputies who accompanied Sheriff McKinny out to the Wood the morning after Hank found Abe and brought him back here."

Shocked, Mike whispered, "The man we spoke to is only twenty-seven years old? My God, I'd have guessed he was closer to sixty."

"Nope," replied the Sheriff as he swiveled his chair around to access the file cabinet immediately behind him. He thumbed through a mass of folders before pulling one file from the drawer. Placing it on the desk before him, he opened it and handed the top page to Mike. It was the notice of report of investigation, including basic information on those involved. The dates and overall information confirmed what the Sheriff had just told him.

Indicating a wooden chair in the corner, the Sheriff said, "You'd better sit down, son. You're looking a mite pale." Mike took his advice, pulling the chair nearer the desk before seating himself. The Sheriff immediately continued.

"I wish I could account for it, but as you must realize by now, Madland County isn't quite like other places and neither are most of the folks who live here. There's something strange about this place, maybe something in the air, the water, the soil or, well, possibly in them all. Things happen here that happen nowhere else, and most of the time those things are bad, sometimes really bad."

"Sheriff, it sounds as if you are about to tell me the story Camden told Jim and I was true, that the soil of this county eats the residents," Mike challenged.

The Sheriff leaned forward intently.

"You can hear what I have to say about what we found that day in the Wood or you can read the official report. It's up to you, my friend."

"Okay," Mike shrugged, "I'm sorry. I'd rather hear it from you, sir."

Relaxing in his seat, the Sheriff smiled encouragingly before continuing.

"Like I said, it was the next morning before we took a ride out to the Wood. Sheriff McKinny and Hank led the way with Tom Riley and me following in a second car. Once Hank showed us where he'd found Roscoe's truck, it wasn't difficult to locate the spot where Abe and the others had climbed the fence. We followed suit, although Hank insisted on remaining outside. It was like a jungle in there, so overgrown that neither fresh air nor much light penetrated the heavy foliage, but we soon found the boys had left a clear trail through the mud and leaves. To make a long story short, it wasn't long before we stumbled upon the skeleton of a man lying on the ground, propped up against a tree.

"Yeah," he added, noting Mike's apparent bewilderment, "just a skeleton. Every bit of flesh, organs, and what have you had been stripped from the bones. Nothing was holding them together but a green-gray fungus that had grown over nearly half of the body. Tom and I put the remains in a body bag we'd brought along, though it wasn't exactly the most pleasant task in the world. Lucky for us, we'd brought gloves along, because the skeleton fell to pieces as soon as it was touched and that fungus wasn't something either one of us wanted to contact directly."

Mike interjected to ask, "Were the remains of an old cabin nearby, maybe three partial walls with a stone floor inside?"

Without pause the Sheriff confirmed that they had encountered an old ruin just a few feet from the corpse.

"Sorry to break in," Mike apologized, "I just remembered Mr. Camden said they'd left Roscoe's body fairly close to a ruined cabin, a leftover from the earliest settlement in the area."

The Sheriff smiled indulgently. "As I recall, we'd pretty much confirmed everything he'd told us before we left, actually more than we would have liked.

"Later, after we got back to town, the doc did an autopsy of sorts on the bones. He claimed he'd never seen anything like it. There were no teeth marks, so no animals had been gnawing on the body, and the only way thing he knew of that could clean a set of bones that quickly would be a strong corrosive, like acid or quicklime, the latter taking days. Either way, nothing would be able to grow on the bones for weeks or months after due to the chemical residue, so he was also at a loss to explain how a fungus could cover so much of the corpse in just a few hours. Sure as hell there wasn't anything natural about it, so we couldn't blame Abe. Hell, the only way we could even be sure it was Roscoe's body was by the gold tooth in the front lower jaw."

"But what about Tuck?" Mike demanded. "If what Camden told us is true, he panicked and left Tuck to die. He claimed he couldn't remember why he'd lost his nerve when he was within inches of rescuing Tuck. That was what really haunted him."

His head lowered, the Sheriff sighed deeply. When he looked up, his entire face seemed to have changed due to his own recollection of that aspect of the story.

"I know. I was coming to that. Poor Abe never stopped torturing himself over Tuck's death despite our desperate attempts to explain what we'd found. Nothing we said or did consoled him. He had to remember that moment for himself, which he never did.

"We found Tuck's body, just as he described it, tied to a tree limb with his own belt. It was dangling from that limb just a few yards from the fence."

He fell silent for a moment, then he raised the file from his desk and handed it to Mike.

"We took photos of both bodies before removing them. The photos are there, so you can see for yourself what we found."

When Mike made no move to open the file, the other man felt obliged to describe what he wished he could forget.

"As we saw it, when Tuck ordered Abe to leave and save himself, Tuck already knew he was a dead man. It wasn't until the boughs parted that Abe saw enough to understand, and what he saw was enough to drive any man mad.

"As the photos show, only half of Tuck came up out of the swampy soil. I can't explain how he held on long enough to warn Abe, but he did. But whatever he'd sunk into had already gotten to him. There was nothing left of his body from the rib cage down; the entire lower half of his body had been eaten away, bone and all.

"That's what Abe saw and that's what caused him to run away. I don't know if he let on about how he and Tuck felt about each other, but everyone knew they loved each other; that's not something we frown upon around here. So keep that in mind when you consider what that moment must have been like for Abe, to see Tuck half gone and ordering him to go. If you can look at it that way, then I think you can understand why he couldn't live with that memory. He did his best by blotting it from his conscious mind, but deep down it was still there."

An ominous silence followed until Mike finally whispered, "He's dead, isn't he? Mr. Camden, I mean."

The Sheriff lowered his head as he nodded in confirmation. "Yeah, he's dead. He put the business end of a shotgun in his mouth three days ago and pulled the trigger. I guess he just couldn't take it anymore."

"And our visit was the last straw. He begged us for help, yet Jim all but spit in his face. I'm no better, though, because I just sat there and let him do it."

At that point, the Sheriff reached across the desk to Mike, placing his hands on top of Mike's.

"When you first told me about your visit and how your buddy went off on Abe, I confess I thought the same thing, son, but now that I've relived the whole thing in my mind, I recall something Abe said to me. We'd already shown him the photos, hoping to convince him he was not responsible for Tuck's death, but he remained inconsolable."

"What did he say?" Mike asked reluctantly.

"He said he could see how the three of us could go into the Wood to fetch the bodies and get out without being affected since it was daytime and we were only there for a short time. What he didn't understand was how he, unlike Roscoe and Tuck, had escaped the Wood's unquenchable hunger. He couldn't understand why it hadn't overtaken him as well."

Mike stared solemnly at the officer, unsure of his point.

"Don't you see? He didn't escape the Wood's ravenous hunger any more than the others did. It ate Roscoe and Tuck right then and there, but it got inside Abe somehow without his knowing it, and it remained there, slowly eating away at his mind during all the years that followed. I'd like to think he finally realized that in the end, so it wasn't himself he killed, it was the ravenous, cancerous hunger that fed on his brain day and night that he was determined to kill when he pulled that trigger. It was the only way for him to free himself and finally find some real peace."

THE GREEN THUMB

John Gregory Betancourt

The sleigh bells on the front door jangled when I went into Debarre's Rare Books. Old Edward Debarre looked up over his half-moon reading glasses and frowned at me. He always did that whenever anyone came into his bookstore, I knew. Definitely *creepy*. That helped explain why he seldom had customers. That, and the fact that rare as his books purported to be, nobody really wanted them. He didn't specialize in mysteries or Americana or even great literature. No, he specialized in the odd and unpopular. A first edition (1890) of *Birds Shown to the Children* had been my only purchase in three years of occasional visits to his shop. That particular book was unremarkable in any way, except that it had a mediocre color plate illustrating sedge-warblers, and I'd been involved in a dispute with my neighbor, June Akoras, over the local existence of those particular birds. I had been right, as the illustration clearly proved. Well worth the $10.60 (including tax) I'd invested in that volume.

Behind me, Debarre cleared his throat. That was the first sound I'd ever heard him utter, except for the price of the bird book I'd bought last year. I felt a chill go down my back. *Don't look*, something inside me said. *Whatever you do, don't look.*

"You like plants?" he asked. His voice was high and wheezy, like an asthmatic's.

I glanced up at the small hand-printed sign thumbtacked over the section I was browsing: *Horticulture*, it said. He had me.

"Yes," I said. With a mental sigh, I turned around.

Debarre was rummaging under the counter. Finally he pulled out a thin book—perhaps thirty or forty pages long—bound in drab olive-green cloth. He set it gingerly on the glass display case, facing it toward me. Then he frowned again.

"What's that?" I asked, peering at it, intrigued despite myself. The book didn't seem to have any lettering stamped on the spine or cover.

"About plants."

"Oh?" I picked it up and carefully opened to the first page. There were a number of dried flowers pressed inside, but that didn't surprise me; lots of old books had them. I'd found roses, baby's breath, even daisies pressed flat in books over the years.

As I leafed forward, the beautiful hand-drawn watercolor illustrations of flowers took my breath away. I recognized Myrtle and Hogswort in the first two-page spread, but the rest—some half a dozen—I didn't know.

The text at the bottom had been hand-set in blocky old type, small but legible. Unfortunately, it wasn't in English . . . German, maybe? Or Dutch? Something with far too many consonants.

I flipped in a few more pages. The

beautiful illustrations continued. This was, I thought, more a work of art than a book. It belonged in a museum. Whoever this long-ago artist had been, his talent was impressive.

Hands trembling, I closed the book and set it down. I wanted it. I wanted it very badly. But I knew I would never be able to afford it. If Debarre charged ten bucks for a beat-up bird book, what would he charge for *this* one? Hundreds, said a little voice inside me. It might as well be thousands, with the meager book-buying budget I allowed myself.

"How much?" I asked. I heard a slight tremor in my voice. Great, I thought, a killer bargaining move. Now he'd *know* I loved the book.

"Twelve dollars, plus tax," he said, still frowning.

"Twelve?" I swallowed. Had I misheard? "Twelve *dollars?*"

He nodded once, almost imperceptibly.

I fumbled my purse open and pulled out a twenty. He plucked it from my fingers, made change from his ancient register, then wrapped my book in brown paper like a fish from the market. I accepted the parcel and hurried out before he could change his mind.

All the way home, I kept expecting to hear footsteps behind me and his wheezing old voice calling, "Hey lady, I made a mistake!"

But by then it would be too late, I thought. The book was mine, and I had no intention of giving it back, mistake or not. I hugged it to my chest. *Mine.*

Nobody chased me. The ten minute walk home proved entirely uneventful. Once I left Main Street, I saw not a living soul, not even June Akoras, my next-door neighbor, who could usually be found working among her prize-winning flowers every Saturday afternoons.

"I hope you get aphids," I told her rose beds as I hurried past.

I took June's absence as a good sign. She beat me every year in the Springfield Gardening Club's "Town Beautiful" Awards, and she liked to gloat and rub my nose in it when she collected her blue ribbons. Invariably, I came in second or third. Worst of all, she always hung her ribbons where I could see them from my kitchen window.

Her wins were a deliberately calculated maneuver. Whatever I planted, she made sure she planted the same thing. She bought the most expensive, exotic, and beautiful varieties available, and as a result hers flowers always outshone mine. I neither forgot nor forgave her for it.

This year we had both planted rosebushes and peonies. With the flower judging coming up in just a few days, I expected her to be out around the clock, puttering, pruning, and fussing over her flowers. And truly they *were* beautiful, the roses huge and heavy, all reds and blushes, the peonies white and red in elegant stripes and swirls.

When I looked at my own peony beds, to either side of my front door, they paled in comparison, weak and spindly, with many small buds and only a scattering of open flowers. My roses, though— there we would have a real competition. This year I had watered and fertilized and pruned and mulched with especial fervor, and my efforts had been rewarded with a luxuriant thatch of roses, a veritable garden hedge between our properties, done all in pink and yellow blossoms. I gave a low but satisfied chuckle. This year we would be evenly matched, I thought.

I carried my slender new book inside my pink-and-white Cape Cod house, where I set it on the kitchen table and unwrapped it carefully.

"I can't believe you're mine," I whispered.

My hands trembled as I opened the first page, spilling pressed flowers out. As with the illustrations, some I recognized and some I did not. All were dried to the point of brittleness. I could have crumbled them all to dust.

Something stopped me from throwing them out, though. They *were* pretty, in an odd sort of way. Perhaps I could make a dried flower arrangement out of them . . .

Again I paged through that slender book, admiring the watercolors. Mistletoe, I recognized, and holly, and wolfbane. It struck me, suddenly, that all the plants I could identify had some sort of mystic connection. I chuckled. Was this a horticulture book, or a witch's guide?

I examined the binding material more closely.

"Odd . . ." I murmured to myself.

The book wasn't bound in cloth, I realized, but something fibrous, like a huge leaf. Running my fingers along the covers, I felt natural ridges and bumps. Not a leaf, exactly, I decided but something like corn husks. I sniffed it, but it just smelled musty, like it had been stored in somebody's attic too long.

It was nearly five o'clock. I'd better start dinner; Jim would be back from the golf club any time now.

Sighing, I pulled an old mixing bowl from the pantry, gathered up all the loose bits and pieces of dried flowers, put them inside, and set the bowl on a high shelf. Tomorrow would be soon enough to deal with *them*, I decided.

Jim didn't understand or particularly like my book-collecting habit, so I took my new trophy into the living room, opened the top shelf of my 4-shelf barrister's bookcase, and slipped it neatly inside. He'd never notice.

•   •   •

Sunday morning, after breakfast, Jim headed off to the golf course again. I got the usual peck on the cheek, the usual mumbled, "Back soon, Hon." I heard the front door slam and the crunch of car wheels on our driveway, and then he was gone.

Sighing, feeling like a perpetual golf widow, I pulled down my old mixing bowl and looked at the dried flowers—what was left of them, anyway. Most of them hadn't survived the night, crumbling to dust while I slept.

I shook my head. Well, you get what you pay for. I hadn't much liked them after all, I told myself.

I was about to dump the whole batch into the garbage when I noticed something small, black, and shiny off to one side of the bowl. It was a seed, I realized as I peered down at it.

Using my thumb and forefinger, I plucked it out and studied it. A seed, but like none I had ever seen before . . . black, shiny like a beetle, and perfectly round except for the tiniest nub on one end. It must have been pressed in the book, too, I thought.

I'd heard of some seeds lasting years. I wondered if this one might sprout.

With a growing sense of excitement, I fetched my new book, opened it, and began searching among the pictures, trying to identify which plant it came from.

An hour later, I had to give up; I just couldn't tell. There were too many pictures, too many unfamiliar plants, and no real illustrations of seeds.

I paused for a second, wondering where to put it. I had a small spot next to the peonies, I finally decided, where it might well grow. There it would get plenty of sun, and I could water it when I watered the rest of the garden.

Nodding, I fetched my gardening fork, gloves, and trowel, then went outside to plant it.

The moment I stepped out my door, I heard a long, loud *Sssss* sound. It was a spray can, I realized, and the sound came from June Akoras's yard.

I peered at her—her, with the orange-frizz hair and that neon orange fingernail polish, looking more like a refuge from clown college that a filthy-rich widow—and suddenly I recognized the bright yellow can she whose contents she was spraying in the air. And then I realized the wind was carrying that spray over the fence and straight toward my roses.

"Stop that!" I screeched, dropping everything and running over.

She stopped spraying and looked at me, a perfect semblance of puzzlement on her face. Oh, but she knew what she was doing, all right. My hatred boiled over.

"You—you—" I began.

"What on *Earth* are you stammering about?" she asked almost sweetly.

I point at the spray can. "That! How could you? *How could you?*"

She looked at the can of wasp spray. "I didn't know you liked the little monsters," she said. "They were buzzing all around the fence, so I thought I'd take

care of them.

"You know perfectly well you can't spray that stuff around plants! It kills them!"

"I'm spraying in my own yard," she said.

"But it's blowing into *mine!*"

"I'm very sorry," she said, half turning and pretending to read the label. One bright orange fingernail tapped with satisfaction on the can. "I'll be more careful."

I stood there and fumed as she retreated toward her house. I had a funny feeling that tomorrow all my roses would be covered with little black dead spots where the mist had landed on them. But what hurt more than that was the look of supreme satisfaction I glimpsed on her face as she slipped inside.

Turning, I looked hopelessly at my roses. All the delicate pinks, the pastel yellows . . . there was no telling how much damage she'd done. Hopefully I'd caught her in time. But I had a distinct feeling I hadn't.

Shaking my head, I headed back toward my house. Only then did I realize I'd dropped that tiny black seed somewhere near my front door. I sighed. So much for that. June had beaten me again.

It probably wouldn't have grown anyway, I told myself. It probably died fifty years ago. Besides, I didn't even know if it was a flower seed.

Somehow, that didn't comfort me one bit. I tried to bury my anger and frustration in weeding and troweling in my peony bed, but I only managed to scare worms and sal bugs, and then I stabbed myself in the finger with my gardening fork.

Yelping, dripping blood, I hurried

into the house. June Akoras had certainly ruined this day for me, I told myself.

•   •   •

After bandaging my finger—luckily, it felt worse than it looked after I rinsed it off and put antiseptic cream on it—I retreated to my kitchen and put the kettle on to boil. A cup of chamomile tea, that's what I needed.

As I waited for the water to boil, I opened that old picture book and again gazed down at the flowers. They were beautiful enough, I thought, that any of them would have beaten June Akoras's garden. Try as I might, I just didn't have the green thumb she did.

Or the spraying index-finger, a dark part of my mind added.

My vision blurred with tears. I would have given anything to beat her this year. *Anything.*

•   •   •

The next morning, after Jim left for the office, I hurried out to check on my roses.

As I expected, half of them were covered with tiny black spots: leaves, flowers, stems. The wasp spray had burned them wherever it landed. They were ruined. Nobody would give me an award this year.

Head down, close to tears, I started back inside. Only then did I notice the change in the peony bed to the left of my front door.

All the peonies had vanished. In the space of a night, every single round red-and-white flower had disappeared, replaced by a luxuriant growth of some splendid russet-leafed plant. Roots spilled out from the flower bed, twining this way and that in the lawn, and leafy runners headed off across my yard in all directions. I even saw one pressed against the basement window almost as though it were peering inside.

"What *are* you?" I asked, bending down to touch one leaf gently.

Something pinched me, and I jerked my hand back. A single drop of blood beaded on my right index finger. Had something stung me? No, I realized, I'd missed the thorns on these strange new plants. Needle-sharp and an inch long, they stuck out all over the stems.

More gently, I parted the leaves.

Then I spotted my peonies. They hung, brown and shriveled, mostly dead, from the thorns. They had been neatly skewered by these new plants. It seemed as though the life had been sucked out of them, but of course that was ridiculous. Plants didn't cannibalize each other, did they?

I sat on my front stoop. As I stared, I noticed small dark buds all over the new thorn plants. Had those buds been there five minutes ago? I hesitated. Nothing grew that fast, I told myself, not even kudzu. No, I'd missed them, like I'd missed the thorns when I'd first looked at the plant. I shook my head. June Akoras had me more rattled than I'd thought.

I studied the runners, heading in every different direction.

"That's where you need to go," I told them, pointing to June's house. "Go suck the life out of her and her rosebushes." I chuckled. It would serve her right, too.

My finger began to throb, so I went back inside. More Band-Aids, more antiseptic cream, and more chamomile tea. This year would be a write-off for the garden club. I'd had a good shot with the roses, but with them gone . . .

I remembered a Desiree Diamond

film festival on TV that afternoon, and I decided to make myself comfortable, curl up with a bowl of popcorn, and try to while away the hours till I had to make dinner for Jim.

The garden club toured on Tuesday, inspecting members' gardens before giving out ribbons. I hadn't a chance in the world this year. But next year . . . yes, next year, I vowed, I'd win once and for all.

• • •

That night, as Jim and I lay spooned together in bed, I dreamed of flowers. I dreamed of that strange plant coming alive, entering the house all over, sending out feelers to investigate. I dreamed that it tickled my nose as it curled protectively about me, about its mistress, about the one who had freed it, the one who had showered blood on it and brought it to life, and we laughed together, my voice melodic, the plant's like the tinkle of wind chimes on a breezy day.

We were one, it an I, of one mind, one body, one voice, and one thought. It became part of me, and together we planned and dreamed. We *would* win that blue ribbon, my familiar and I. It would be easy.

Together we stole into June's garden and sucked the life from her roses. Together we pushed under her back door, sent tendrils into her bedroom, and lifted her—*gently, gently! Don't wake her!*—from her sheets. Together we bore her out and away.

All about my house and garden all the plants danced and sang, and I danced with them, a wild Disneyfied frenzy of green and white and pink and red, and I knew true happiness for the first time in many years.

• • •

When I awakened, I felt curiously refreshed. I no longer cared that June Akoras has maimed my roses. It was a wonderful day, and nothing could spoil it.

After I sent Jim off to work with a huge breakfast of blueberry pancakes under his belt, I ventured outside to check on my thorn-bed. To my surprise I found it beautifully in bloom. Huge pink flowers, some the size of dinner plates, some the size of teacups, and all splashed with deep blood red at the centers, had opened everywhere.

The five judges from the garden club were all standing around, *oohing and aahing.*

"What is it?" one of them asked me. "It's beautiful—I've never seen anything like it. Does it belong to the hibiscus family?"

"Uh, yes, I believe so," I said. The plant looked familiar now that I saw it in bloom; there were several pictures of it in that strange old plant book. "I'm not sure what its common name is. If you'll wait a minute, I can look up its scientific name—"

"We can get to that later," she said. "We just have one more house to look at, but I think I can say with all confidence that you're going to have a ribbon this year."

"A . . . ribbon?" I stared at her, shocked. It was all happening so fast.

"Come, ladies," she said, and she turned and headed for June Akoras's garden.

I trailed them as far as my fence, almost stumbling over a large runner, as big around as a garden hose, from my strange little thorn-plants. This runner went to the edge of my property, then vanished underground. But on the other side of the fence I could see its effects.

Every one of June's beautiful rose plants lay dead or hopelessly withered. Blackened flowers drooped like dead fruit from thin, brown stalks. I had never seen anything so pathetic.

Neither, it seemed, had the garden club. *Tsk-tsk*ing, they checked a few boxes on their clipboards.

I was amazed June hadn't come outside to protest that I'd done something to her roses. She probably didn't have the nerve after what I caught her doing yesterday, I told myself. She was sneakier than that. I was more likely to find her digging up my garden at midnight than trying to persuade the judges I'd bushwhacked her garden.

I went back to my strange new flower bed, gazing down at all the beautiful flowers. As I stood there, half numb with pleasant shock, I glimpsed a bright neon orange something lying on the ground.

No, I thought, bending down to look, it wasn't *on* the ground, it was poking up *through* the ground. It was a pale, bloodless, two-inch length of finger. Its nail had been painted bright orange. From the tip of the finger emerged a plant stalk, one leading to an exception-ally bright and beautiful flower.

I did *not* scream. Instead, I coolly moved by toe, subtly scuffing mulch up to cover that telltale digit.

After all, I couldn't have June ruining my chances to win a ribbon now, I told myself. What would the judges think of a plant growing from a human finger? No, they would not be happy.

I would bury it more deeply later, I decided. And I'd search my garden for any more fingers or toes which might be poking up too conspicuously.

Sighing happily, I knelt by my beautiful thorn-plant. As I reached down to touch it, I sensed its thorns drawing back to protect me. Gently, I began to stroke its russet-colored leaves.

"Good girl," I whispered to it, a proud mother now. "Good, good girl."

•　　•　　•

Later that afternoon, when the garden club presented me with my first blue ribbon—Best Flower Garden—I blushed and stammered.

"I couldn't have done it without June Akoras," I said. "She has always been a source of inspiration."

After all, I realized now, it was her blood that gave the blossoms their deep rich red glow. Secretly, I smiled.

ABOUT THE COVER ARTIST

JASON VAN HOLLANDER has become a modern master of weird and uncanny artwork. He started his career with illustration and design work for Arkham House, and followed up soon after with more exquisite illustration for such magazines as *Weird Tales®, Deathrealm*, and Marion Zimmer Bradley's *Fantasy Magazine*. In addition, he has supplied interior illustrations for Joan Aiken's *The Cockatrice Boys* (Tor 1996), Fritz Leiber's *The Dealings of Daniel Kesserich* (Tor 1997), and (with Darrell Schweitzer) wrote and designed the brilliant short story collection *Necromancies & Netherworlds* (nominated for a World Fantasy Award). An excellent introduction to his black and white illustration would be the recommended portfolio *De Morbis Aritificum*.

In 2000, Jason won a World Fantasy Award for Best Artist. He has also published fiction in *Fantasy Magazine* and *Weird Tales®*.

Prints and portfolios of his work are available. For more information, email: magicpenjvh@msn.com.

www.ingramcontent.com/pod-product-compliance
Lightning Source LLC
Chambersburg PA
CBHW072011170626

46813CB00005B/2107